MASARU

MASARU

勝

by
Michael T. Cibenko

Arx Publishing
Merchantville, New Jersey
2021

Arx Publishing
Merchantville, New Jersey

First Edition

ISBN: 978-1-935228-23-3

For Eric
The quest for the perfect warrior
leads to the heart of Christ.

INTRODUCTION

Christianity came to the islands of Japan when Spanish missionary, St. Francis Xavier, arrived with a small group of Jesuits in 1549. At that time, the country was in the throes of the Warring States era, a century-long period of civil conflict in which feudal lords (*daimyō*) vied for centralized control over the islands. Further complicating matters was the rise of the *sōhei*, a sect of Buddhist monk warriors who opposed the feudal system altogether. In the midst of this social and political maelstrom, the formerly centralized power of the emperor was diluted. Such was the state of affairs when Francis and his companions landed on the shores of Kagoshima in the southernmost island of Kyūshū.

Life during this period was especially difficult for the peasants, who endured poverty and much suffering. It may have been in part for this reason that they were so receptive to the Gospel message of hope, peace, and salvation. Evangelization in the beginning, however, was not without difficulty, mainly owing to language and cultural barriers. (For example, the word "*Dainichi*," initially used to refer to the one true God, also happened to be the name of a Buddhist deity.) Such obstacles would eventually be overcome, and the conversion of many commoners followed. Even several feudal lords, particularly in the southern regions, became practitioners of the new religion that came to be known as *Kirisutokyō*. Over the next roughly fifty years, the number of Christians grew to over three hundred thousand.

By the early 17th century, all of Japan was finally unified under the military and political rule of Ieyasu Tokugawa, the man who claimed the title of *shōgun*. Owing to the generally held Shintō belief that the emperor was a direct descendant of the sun goddess, Amaterasu, it would not have been prudent for the *shōgun* to usurp the emperor's power. Instead, the emperor would retain his nominal role as head of state, while Tokugawa wielded all practical power and authority.

Christianity, which had been tolerated up to that point, came under increasingly hostile treatment with each successor of the Tokugawa clan. They viewed the religion, and foreign influences in general, as a threat to national sovereignty. A campaign to rid the islands of *Kirisutokyō* began in the capital city of Kyōto, and would eventually make its way to the southernmost part of the country where Francis and his companions had first landed. The thousands of believers inhabiting that region, who had every intention of passing along the teachings of Christ to their children, would be in for a rude awakening.

A NOTE ON THE JAPANESE LANGUAGE

The reader will notice the frequent occurrence of Japanese words and phrases throughout the text. The pronunciation of Japanese, particularly when compared to other Asian languages, is relatively straightforward. As I used to tell my students, if you get the vowels right, everything else more or less falls into place. For reference, the vowels of Japanese are essentially pronounced the same as those of Italian. Think of words like "amore" and "Luigi."

The Japanese "a" is always pronounced in short form, as in "father," as opposed to "acorn". The "e" is also pronounced in short form, as in "egg," as opposed to "equal." An "e" at the end of a word should be voiced accordingly. This is why the correct pronunciation of the word "karate," for example, sounds more like "kara-tay" than "kara-tee." The Japanese "i" is voiced like a long "e," as in "piano," as opposed to "ivy". The "o" is also pronounced in long form, as in "old," as opposed to "olive."

The appearance of a line over a vowel, such as with the name of the main character, "Shirō," does not change the voicing of that vowel. It does, however, lengthen the sound of that vowel. In musical terms, it's somewhat like lengthening an eighth note to a quarter note. Therefore, the main character's name, correctly pronounced, sounds something like, "Shee-roh," with the final vowel extended slightly. While this may perhaps seem frivolous, it should be noted that the length of a vowel can determine the meaning of words. For example, the word "oji-san" means "uncle," whereas "ojī-san" means "grandfather." Similarly, "oba-san" means "aunt," while "obā-san" means "grandmother."

GLOSSARY

Most of the numerous Japanese words and phrases used throughout *Masaru* are easily understood from context. When the phrase is especially long or the meaning is more obscure, a translation is provided in a footnote on the same page.

For all Japanese words and phrases used throughout *Masaru*, an English translation may be found in the glossary provided at the end of the book.

JAPAN
of the
17th Century, AD

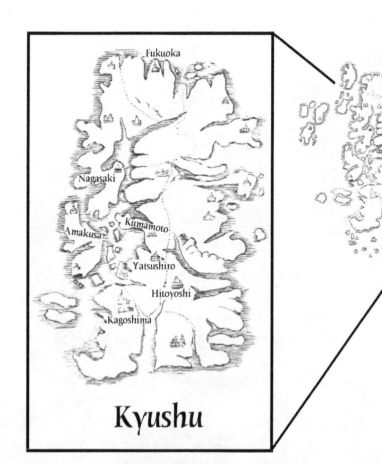

Fukuoka

Nagasaki

Amakusa

Kumamoto

Yatsushiro

Hitoyoshi

Kagoshima

Kyushu

Hokkaido

Honshu

Shikoku

Kyoto

Kobe
Osaka
Hiroshima
Nara

Nagoya

Edo

MASARU

一

CROSSING WATERS
川を渡る

*"Unless a grain of wheat falls to the ground and dies,
it remains just a grain of wheat. But if it dies,
it produces much fruit."*
John 12:24

*"Be like wheat whereas the taller you grow, the lower
you bow your head to the ground."*
Japanese proverb

The warm drops upon his head brought Shirō back to the moment of his baptism. He and his mother had received the rite of Christian initiation on the very same day in the small church near the headwaters of the Kuma River. It was six months after her thirty-third birthday, and five months after his sixteenth. Ritual had been nothing new to Shirō. In the first month of that same year, he had gone through the *genpuku*, the rite of passage in which a *samurai* received his helmet, armor, and sword. The meticulously crafted and deadly *katana*—along with its shorter companion, the *wakizashi*—was more than a weapon. It was an extension of a warrior's soul.

Shirō Nakagawa was, in many ways, very much like any other boy growing up in the rural region of central Kyūshū, the southernmost of Japan's main islands. He enjoyed the company of friends, and afternoons spent fishing along the banks of the Kuma. He was tall for his age, a characteristic about which he was more self-conscious than proud. He had a tendency to slouch slightly, something that his grandmother, Obāsan, was continually correcting. She would poke him with one bony finger in the back, just hard enough to cause a little discomfort, and chide him saying, "*Shisei, shisei!*—Posture, posture!"

He believed himself too skinny, and attempted in vain to gain weight by eating *onigiri* rice balls as quickly as Obāsan or his mother could make them. He even tried to get them to make *chanko nabe*, the protein-rich stew consumed in large quantities by the *sumo* wrestlers of Edo, Nagoya, Osaka, and Fukuoka. But meat was not so easy to come by. Neither the rice balls nor his daily ritual of physical training did much to add girth to his slender frame, a trait he had inherited from his mother. Still, he was healthy and strong, and while generally regarded as attractive, there was an almost feminine quality to the features of his face. In this regard also, he had the look of his mother about him. From the age of twelve, he had allowed his hair to grow, and he wore it most times in a ponytail that he kept tied high at the back of his head.

Shirō was in many ways like the other boys in his village of Watari, but not in all ways. He liked to spend considerable time—perhaps inordinate time—by himself. Many mornings he would wander off to one of the hillsides, simply to walk and be alone with his thoughts, or find an isolated meadow where he would lie and stare up at the clouds. Though his family harbored some degree of concern about him, Shirō always made sure to be home before dark and in time for *bangohan*, the evening meal.

His father, Hiromu Nakagawa, was of the warrior class

and served under Lord Yanazume, master of Hitoyoshi Castle and its surrounding lands. Yanazume had become one of the many converts to the new religion that arrived with the men from Spain and Portugal on the big ships with their billowing sails. They arrived with the man called Francis in the year called 1549 by the *Kirishitans*, the twenty-third year in the reign of the emperor Tomohito, some seventy years before Shirō was born. Upon his own conversion, Yanazume had encouraged all his subjects to become followers of The Way, and they did so by the thousands. He had even enjoined all warriors wishing to remain in his service to be baptized. Should they choose not to, they would be fairly compensated before being released.

At thirty-five years of age, Hiromu had no desire to become *rōnin*—a *samurai* wandering in search of a master. And so he chose, along with two-thirds of the nearly seven hundred *samurai* serving under Yanazume, to become a practitioner of The Way. He wished at the time that his decision had been driven by some noble ideal. But the truth was that he was prompted by the practical need to provide for his family, and he would soon have another small mouth to feed. Perhaps that reason was noble enough.

But practicality did not come without a price. In the beginning, Hiromu's wife was not pleased with his decision to accept the foreign religion brought to their shores by *gaijin*, the "outside ones." Hiromu had half-jokingly pointed out that since her name, Michiko, literally meant "child of the way," perhaps this was some sort of sign. But she was not so easily convinced. Far less pleased was Obāsan, who had lived with Shirō and his parents until her passing. Obāsan was a devout Buddhist and very much set in her ways. Every day, Shirō would hear her reciting chants outside in the garden or before the small *butsudan* shrine in their home, or observe her meditating before a smoldering stick of incense.

One evening during *bangohan*, when Shirō was about eleven, Obāsan let her feelings be known. She addressed her son-in-law, "Hiromu, I cannot understand for the life of me why anyone would profess this foreign faith. I've been looking into it, and some of the things these *Kirishitans* believe are simply outlandish!"

Obāsan had a robustness of character that belied her small stature and slight frame. Though in her sixth decade, she still had a thick head of long raven hair with only streaks of silver along the temples. Her face had few wrinkles, most visibly small crow's feet at the corners of the eyes, and was dotted with several small dark moles, the most noticeable just between her right upper lip and cheek. One vertical crease down the middle of her forehead became pronounced when she was cross, as she was at this particular moment.

Hiromu gave a half-suppressed laugh in his deep booming voice. It was a voice that Shirō both admired and feared. Very few were the times in Shirō's childhood that his father needed to raise a hand to him. His imposing stature and the power of his voice were sufficient to remind Shirō of expected parameters and potential consequences. Hiromu had taught his son many things, including the art of the sword and how to ride a horse. He was a good teacher and a loving father, though there were times when Shirō did stretch the limits of his patience.

"Yes, Obāsan," replied Hiromu. "I cannot wholly disagree with that charge. But in fairness, *Bukkyō* also came here from foreign shores."

Obāsan was indignant. "Well, that's different! Those who brought it were at least of a kindred race. Besides, the deities of *Bukkyō* pair up logically with the nature *kami* of our native Shintō. The *Kirishitans* worship the image of a dead man."

"It is not the image they worship—it is the man. And though He died, He now lives. We believe that man to be the one true God incarnate."

"And why would this God desire to become a man?"

"In Shintō there is the belief that the spiritual manifests itself in the natural world. *Kirisutokyō* professes something even greater—that the one true God, the creator of time and space and all that inhabit them, humbled Himself to become one of his own creation."

"To what end? To be killed by his own creatures?"

"He allowed himself to be sacrificed for the atonement of sins, yes. Beyond that, he conquered death by rising again from the grave."

Obāsan shook her head. "None of it makes sense to me. And what of the belief about eating this man's flesh and blood? I've never heard anything so preposterous!"

Hiromu scraped the remnants of rice from his bowl into his mouth with his long wooden *hashi*. "Obāsan, I may not yet be sufficiently learned to make all these things clear. You should come with us one Sunday to *Misa* and speak to Olivera-san. He is far better than I at explaining these things."

Obāsan recoiled at the sound of the name. "I have no use for your priests. The *bonze* at the temple warned me to stay away from them."

Though he would not openly say as much, Shirō enjoyed these occasional clashes between his father and Obāsan. Aside from the amusement of seeing Obāsan get rather riled, they gave Shirō much to ponder as he lay at night upon his *futon*, before sleep would overtake him. Shirō very much loved his Obāsan in spite of her many quirks and eccentricities, and perhaps even more because of them.

From the time he was a small child, she called him by

the pet name of Masaru. His real name, Shirō, meant simply "fourth son," and was given because he was the fourth male child of his generation. (He had three older male cousins, the sons of his father's elder brother.) The first syllable of his given name, *shi*, meant "four," but also happened to be a homophone for "death." Though the written characters were distinct from one another, still the spoken pronunciation was the same. Obāsan, being superstitious, didn't care for names containing that sound. Shirō was only two or three when he first asked her what the name Masaru meant. She looked at him with wide eyes and uttered the single word, "Victory."

Over time, Hiromu came to realize that being a disciple of Iesu entailed much more than adherence to a weekly ritual. It demanded a change to nearly every facet of one's existence, and even an altogether different understanding of reality itself. But, for his part, Hiromu took considerable pains not to force The Way upon his family.

He recalled from his own childhood the excitement he once experienced upon seeing a full and radiant rainbow after a torrential downpour during the annual season of *tsuyu*. He stood outside and called with great excitement until his parents and siblings came running out of the house to see what all the fuss was about. He hoped that The Way might be something akin to that rainbow, something whose compelling beauty, a splendor too great not to be shared, might draw his family out from the comfortable confines of their own certainties.

And eventually this did happen. To Hiromu's joy (and much to Obāsan's chagrin), Michiko and Shirō together had agreed to be baptized. For Michiko, the decision was at least partly born of a desire to please her husband and to maintain harmony in the home. For Shirō there was something in the teachings of The Way that stimulated his intellect. This was also true of the teachings of *Bukkyō*, with which Shirō had become quite familiar. The Four Noble Truths, for example, offered insight into the nature of suffering that was difficult to dispute.

But there always seemed something lacking, something about *Bukkyō* that did not ultimately satisfy. Perhaps it was the perpetual looking inward and a preoccupation with self in the quest for *nehan*. *Kirisutokyō* also held as a principal aim the attainment of a particular state, namely a "state of grace." But this state was inextricably and beautifully bound to an intimate relationship with an actual person. Where *Bukkyō* concerned itself with the questions of "what" and "how," everything in *Kirisutokyō* flowed from the understanding and friendship of a "who."

Shirō had spent the previous year studying medicine on the island of Amakusa to the west. When he first approached his parents about this vocation, his father was dubious. Hiromu put the question rhetorically to his son, "How can someone be both a warrior and a healer?"

But Shirō replied, "Was not Iesu both?" With that answer, Hiromu had little choice but to bestow his blessings.

Some days before their baptism, Shirō and Michiko were in the house as she made the usual *bangohan* preparations. She was a tall and slender woman, with signs that she was with child only just beginning to show beneath the folds of her loosely fitting *yukata* robe. From the v-line of her *yukata* rose her long neck, like the stem of a chalice, the bowl of which was formed by the round smoothness of her jawline. Her full lips and high bridge of the nose were crowned with a pair of kind eyes that, if one looked just a little deeper, conveyed a sense of sadness and longing. Shirō, washing his hands in a small basin, called to his mother, "Okāsan, you know we're soon to be baptized. Perhaps we should get in a little practice!" With that, he took a scoop of water in his hands and splashed it playfully onto her face.

She stood frozen for a moment as the water dripped down her neck and into her *yukata*. "You rascal! I'll give you some practice!" Grabbing a wooden spoon from a bowl of utensils, she chased him out of the house, both of them laughing. Some neighbors looked up momentarily from their gardening and shook their heads.

"Do you understand why baptism is necessary?" Father Olivera had put this question to Shirō as they walked through the nearby woods of Ishino, as they had on so many occasions. Shirō became acquainted with Father Olivera, the man he called Shinpu, shortly after his father's conversion. Manuel Olivera was a ruggedly handsome man. His dark features might have allowed him to be mistaken for one of the native population, if not for the thick wavy hair and full but neatly-trimmed beard, both of which were beginning to show distinguished streaks of gray. Shirō very much enjoyed their talks, and he appreciated that Shinpu always spoke to him in an adult manner.

"Yes," replied Shirō, "My father explained it to me." Hiromu had indeed told Shirō the story of the first man and woman in the garden of perfection, and of the circumstances and consequences of their disobedience. The effects of their choice would be passed along to their offspring and the entire human race. A spiritual defect, not necessarily visible to the eye but just as real as any physical flaw, would be the inheritance of all. All but one.

Though Shirō found the tale intriguing, the reality of shared dishonor was not something unfamiliar to him. When he was a child, one of his cousins had stolen a *mikan* orange from a vendor in a neighboring village. Returning home and discovering the small item in the boy's possession, his parents, along with the grandparents, aunts, uncles, and all the cousins, including Shirō, made the two-hour-long trek back to the merchant to return the item and beg forgiveness. Shirō understood well that even small transgressions could bring shame and dishonor not only upon oneself, but to one's entire tribe.

"There is one thing I do not understand," said Shirō.

"Oh? And what is that?"

"Why was it necessary for Iesu to be baptized? If he is truly divine, he could have no sin to cleanse."

"Very true. But it was for our sake, not his, that Iesu was baptized. The baptisms performed by John were a sign of repentance. But when Iesu entered the river, the waters of baptism through all space and time were sanctified."

Shirō pondered that for a moment. "You mean his *ki* entered into the water?" *Ki* was the word used to describe the energy or life force of a living being. From the time Shirō was a small boy, greater awareness and focus of *ki* was always at the heart of his training in the fighting arts.

Father Olivera smiled. "Something like that, yes."

11

The waters of the Kuma River crept lazily in the warmth of the early afternoon. In another season, one might have seen through the crystalline water, right down to the smooth round stones that lined its bottom and the abundant *ayu* fish darting about in search of food. But the *kōyō* season had just surpassed its peak. Now this section of the river was covered with a blanket of fallen maple leaves, moving almost imperceptibly and shimmering in the mid-November sun. It appeared from a distance like a silken sash of crimson, separating the dancing brown plumes of miscanthus on either side.

From the dense forest along the river's western bank emerged a dark figure. By the silhouette of its thick body, six legs, and two long prongs projecting from its head, it appeared like a giant *kabuto-mushi*, the rhinoceros beetle common in the broad-leaved forests of Kyūshū. Lord Onizuka, in full battle armor and perched atop his satiny black stallion, surveyed the river. He and a battalion of three hundred strong had made the two-day trek on horseback and foot from the castle in Yatsushiro to the north. Onizuka and his men had camped the previous night beside a small Shintō shrine at the river's edge. The shrine was dedicated to Inari, goddess of rice and fertility, and Onizuka used the occasion to pray that his mission bear fruit.

In the time of Onizuka's grandfather, the new religion had arrived along with the traders who sailed into Nagasaki from the faraway Iberian peninsula. And for a long time, it was generally tolerated by the military and political authorities. In exchange for allowing the *Kirishitan* missionaries to build places of worship and make converts, the feudal lords reaped the benefits of trade made possible by the big ships of the *gaijin*. As an added benefit, the arrival of the new religion, it was hoped, might counteract the growing influence of the

Buddhist monks, whose numbers and opposition to *samurai* rule were threatening to become more than a nuisance.

But what was originally perceived as a benign though misguided belief system had become an even more potentially serious threat. What no one could have predicted was the spread like wildfire of the Christian *hukuin*, what they called "the good news," among all the classes—peasant, warrior, merchant, and noble alike. It began as something of a regional phenomenon in the port areas of the south, but before long it had made its way to nearby Shikoku and deep into the main island of Honshū. It was widely feared that the infusion of this foreign belief system, along with its allegiance to a foreign figurehead, might upend social and political stability. Some believed this may have been the aim of Spain's King Philip all along.

One final straw was the growing agitation stemming from recent reports that some of the Portuguese traders were taking peasants and selling them as slaves in the Spanish territories of mainland Asia. The *shōgun* had finally had enough. He ordered the closing of all Christian churches and missions, the expulsion of the priests, and a ban of all Christian practices and images.

Onizuka was certainly the right man for the task at hand, and he'd been appointed by Lord Iemitsu Tokugawa himself—the man who assumed the title of *shōgun* from his father and predecessor, Hidetada. Though the elder Tokugawa had tried to discourage the growing Christian population by means of heavy taxation, it proved to be insufficient in stemming the tide of conversions. Now the younger Tokugawa was determined to use more direct and, if necessary, brutal means.

At twenty-six years of age, Onizuka had ample experience in the tactics of warfare, both on and off the open battlefield.

He was full of ambition and fire coursing through his veins. He had little love for the Buddhists, and even less for the followers of *Kirisuto*, for whom he harbored a particular disdain. He loathed the absurdity of the worship of a simple peasant man turned rebel and insurrectionist. That the image of this man nailed to a beam could be their symbol of hope and salvation defied all dignity and reason. He had never approved of the past permissiveness in allowing the foreigners to spread their pious poison. Now he was all too happy to assist in the administration of the antidote.

Raising his sword toward the opposite shore, Onizuka urged his horse forward through a shallow stretch of the river. The small village of Kōnose lay waiting idly on the other side. The entire battalion, those on horse followed by those on foot, charged after him into and across the water, churning the still blanket of red into a swirling gray mire of sludge.

二

MATTER AND MASS
物質と質量

*"Things are not always what they seem; outward form
deceives many; rare is the mind that discerns what is
carefully concealed within."*
Plato, The Phaedrus

"A frog in the well knows nothing of the great sea."
Japanese proverb

"Are you ready to receive the Blessed Sacrament?" Father
Olivera put this question to Shirō as they walked the
path that meandered alongside the Kuma River. Now that
Shirō and his mother were baptized, they would be able to
fully participate in the memorial of the Lord's Supper. Father
Olivera took the opportunity on this day to see if his young
friend understood what this meant. A warm breeze caught
the loose folds of the priest's cassock, making the sleeves
billow and flap about like the *koi nobori* banners flown on
festival days.

He had first arrived in Japan when he was only a few years
older than Shirō. He'd felt a calling to the priesthood, as well

15

as adventure, from an early age. When the Society of Jesus opened Japan's first seminary on the island of Amakusa, just south of Nagasaki, young Manuel jumped at the opportunity. Upon his ordination, Father Olivera was assigned to the inland city of Hitoyoshi and all the outlying villages in the Kuma region. Over time, the language and customs of the converts he served, now well into the thousands, became as familiar to him as those of his native Portugal.

"I am not certain," replied Shirō. "It is a hard thing to believe. I have been coming to *Misa* for many months now. I see the *pan*. I do not see that it is anything other than *pan*."

Father Olivera looked up at Shirō, and then turned his gaze again upon the path. "Yes, well, that is certainly something worth considering." They continued a short distance until they came to the small Shintō shrine they often passed on their walks. At the entrance stood the customary *torī*, the bright crimson wooden structure of two vertical posts and two horizontal crossbeams, the gateway representing the transition from the mundane to the sacred. At the river's edge, a small fishing boat lay moored to a nearby maple tree. Father Olivera went over to the tree and, placing his hands upon it, he asked Shirō, "What do we call this?"

"What do you mean?"

"What is the word for this thing I am touching?"

"You know it is called *ki*." Shirō might have wondered about such a childlike question, but he knew Father Olivera well enough to know that his questions always had some purpose.

"And what is the actual stuff of which *ki* is made?"

Shirō pondered this for a moment before answering with the Japanese word for wood. "*Moku?*"

"Yes, *moku*. So, you agree we can say that *moku* is the stuff of which *ki* is made?"

"There are other parts, such as the leaves, but yes, I do agree."

Following the length of rope to the empty boat, Father Olivera asked in a similar way, "And what do we call this?"

"You know it is called *fune*," replied Shirō, speaking the word for boat.

"Indeed. And what is the stuff of which the *fune* is made?"

"It, too, is made of *moku*."

"We know this to be true. We even know the man who cut down and hollowed out the tree to make it. And, having done so, he now has something quite different from that with which he began."

"Yes," Shirō agreed. "*Ki* and *fune* are quite distinct from one another."

"And yet both are *moku*." Father Olivera stepped away from the river's edge and back toward the shrine's entrance along the path. "And what about the *torī*? Was it not also constructed from *ki* taken from the forest?"

"Yes," answered Shirō. "I agree with all you say, though I do not understand what any of this has to do with the *pan* and the Blessed Sacrament."

"My young friend, my question is this. If man, himself a creature and limited in his powers, can transform a thing into something else, while the very substance of the thing remains the same, would it not also be possible that God, the author of all creation and whose powers have no limitation, could change the substance of a thing while its form and all appearances remain the same?"

Shirō stood by the water's edge, gazing at the full moon. It was not nearly as big or bright as it had been at the time of *tsukimi*, the previous month's harvest moon. But in its perfect and white circularity, he could see the image of the consecrated hosts lying scattered upon the *tatami* floor.

That morning, as he had every Sunday since his baptism, Shirō accompanied his parents to *Misa*. It was to be the first time that he and his mother would receive the Blessed Sacrament. After the previous day's conversation with Father Olivera, Shirō came to the conclusion that he could indeed believe something even without comprehending it fully. After all, the natural world was filled with wonders that, though undeniable in their reality, still presented a sense of mystery and awe. He could not, for example, fully grasp the invisible and universal force that caused a stone released from his hand to fall to the ground. Yet he knew that force to be just as real as the stone itself and even his very own hand.

The church of Saint Michael was not a particularly large structure. It had been built when Shirō was still a toddler, and was situated halfway between Watari village and the northern border of the fairly sizable town of Hitoyoshi. It was hoped that one day a larger cathedral might be erected in the heart of Hitoyoshi itself. Shirō had heard of the colossal stone cathedrals of Europe, constructions that dwarfed even the great temple of Tōdai-ji in Nara. He hoped it might be possible for him to see one of them with his own eyes someday. Shirō was grateful that he at least had been able to visit the churches of Amakusa, Nagasaki, Yastushiro, and even Kumamoto. While each had an unmistakable ornate quality (the manner of Spanish and Portuguese dress was likewise quite something to behold), yet each had its own distinctive character, and was carefully designed to complement its natural surroundings.

Though modest in size and simple in its construction, the church of Saint Michael was quite unlike the other buildings of the village. Rising up from its roof was a steeple of about twelve *shaku* in height, and adorned with a cross of *hinoki* cypress, crafted by Ichiro Kimura, a village artist and convert.

Stepping into the church's front entrance, Shirō removed his sandals in the *genkan*, and placed them into one of several small cubicles before entering the church proper. He then took seat between his parents on one of the *tatami* mats positioned on either side of a narrow aisle leading to a long rail with an altar behind it. The other worshippers, nearly one hundred in number, were already seated or just taking their places. They greeted one another in silence with gentle bows of the head. Shirō knew everyone by face if not by name. Though most were citizens of Hitoyoshi, many others, including Shirō and his parents, made the walk from Watari and other surrounding villages.

It had become evident in recent years that there were not enough priests to meet the growing demand for the administering of the sacraments. There were days when Father Olivera would hear confessions from morning until nightfall without taking time even to eat. The rapid spread of the religion was a phenomenon that no one could quite explain, but it held a distinct appeal to each of the classes. And at the heart of that appeal was not so much its doctrines and rituals (although that was certainly no small part), but rather the person of Iesu himself, who embodied the essence of all the classes—King, warrior, teacher, carpenter's son. And to all was offered a meaning for suffering in this life, and the hope of eternal happiness in the next. And now young men were beginning to enter the seminaries. Shirō had even contemplated the possibility of the priesthood for himself.

At the front and center of the church was a large wooden crucifix with the image of *Kirisuto* nailed upon it—the arms outstretched and the head, adorned with a crown of thorns, hung low. Whenever Shirō gazed upon it, he found himself imagining the arrest of Iesu in the garden, and how the apostle—the one called Iwa—drew his sword to defend Iesu, even cutting off the ear of one of the soldiers. Shirō often wondered what he would have done had he been present in that faraway garden on that fateful night. Though Iesu reprimanded Iwa for his actions, Shirō knew in his heart that he would have done the same.

Directly beneath the foot of the cross stood the tabernacle in which the Blessed Sacrament was housed. To the left of the cross and slightly recessed within the wall, was a small statue of Maria, the mother of Iesu. In a corresponding position to the right of the cross stood a statue of Joseph, the carpenter from Nazareth and earthly father of Iesu. Along the side walls of the church were long narrow windows of stained glass depicting scenes from the life of *Kirisuto*. And inside the church's entrance, just beyond the *genkan*, was a small statue, carved from a solid piece of cypress, of the church's namesake. These items and more had been brought by missionaries from Spain and Portugal. Many of them, as Father Olivera had told Shirō, had been blessed by the Holy Father Urban in distant Rome.

One piece of art in the church that had not been imported was a painting done by Ichiro Kimura, the village artisan. Ichiro had once been shown a print of a painting from a hundred years earlier by an Italian artist named Raphael. The painting depicted the archangel Michael engaged in battle with the fallen angel, Lucifer. Ichiro was inspired to recreate the painting, but he rendered Michael as a *samurai* dressed in full battle armor, and wielding a *katana*, raised and ready to strike. Lucifer was depicted as an undersea serpent, its black tongue dangling from its wide mouth agape—its bulging eyes fixed on the sword poised to fall upon it. One of the angel warrior's feet, planted upon the monster's throat, steadied the beast for the fatal blow. In the background was a dark blue sky filled with stars and the large white perfect circle of a full moon, all conveying the cosmic proportions of this battle between forces of good and evil.

Shirō's attention was drawn away from the details of the church interior when a young woman entered with her parents and two younger brothers. She appeared to glide across the *tatami* floor, as the length of her *kimono* hid from view the small graceful steps of her feet. In some ways, she reminded Shirō of a younger version of his own mother, but with features that were even softer. Her face had a nearly perfect roundness that was accentuated by long hair held in place atop her head with a single *kanzashi* stick. Some strands of hair ran diagonally across her forehead and along the nape of her neck, creating an appearance like that of a veil. But it was her eyes that prompted recognition in Shirō. Her name was Kumiko, a girl he had known since childhood. He had not seen her since the time he had left for his studies on Amakusa. At that time she was still something of a clumsy girl. Now he could see she was becoming a beautiful young woman.

When they had been about ten years old, one of the older boys, a local bully, had taken away Kumiko's doll. She cried and tried desperately to get it back, but the boy teased her mercilessly and threw the toy roughly back and forth with some of his friends. Seeing Kumiko in such distress moved young Shirō to act without thinking. He attacked the bigger, stronger boy, and paid a considerable price for it. After whipping Shirō pretty soundly, the boy threw the doll down

21

in the dirt beside him. Then he mocked him saying, "You like girl dolls so much? Here, play with it, Masaru-chan!" Then he and his friends strode off laughing.

Kumiko walked over to Shirō, now sitting up on the ground, his lower lip swollen and bleeding. He held up the doll for her, and she received it with a soft smile and bow of gratitude. "*Dōmo arigatō*, Shirō-kun." She kissed him gently on his cheek and went back home to nurse her doll. Shirō always remembered the tender touch of her lips and the penetrating look of compassion in her chestnut eyes.

Shirō was drawn out of his childhood memory as the readings began. Upon their arrival in Nagasaki, the Society of Jesus had brought with them, among other things, Japan's first printing press. This allowed for each Christian family to have a book of prayers to bring to *Misa* each week. However, the sacred readings were given voice by Father Olivera from the one large and weighty *Seisho* that was kept in the church. The stories and the characters were rich with drama. The settings were sometimes exotic, sometimes desolate. The plots took unexpected twists and turns. Yet always there was something wonderful and mysterious toward which all was directed.

The first reading that day was about the people of Israel in the desert after they had escaped their Egyptian captors. They were without food and starving, and God provided them with a strange form of sustenance called manna that fell upon the ground from heaven. Shirō wondered how this manna might have tasted. This was followed by a reading from the gospel of John in which Iesu spoke of himself as the "bread of life," telling his disciples that the bread was his flesh, and that they must eat it. Many of his disciples found this teaching too much to bear and would no longer follow him.

"It is time now," Hiromu whispered to signal the moment had arrived to receive the Blessed Sacrament. Everyone stood and slowly processed to the long wooden rail before the altar. They knelt at the rail and waited as Father Olivera went from one end to the other, gently placing the small flat host into their open mouths. It made Shirō think of baby birds in a nest, their blind eyes closed and mouths open wide, waiting for their mother to provide what they cannot themselves attain.

Father Olivera, standing before Shiro's mother as she tipped her head back slightly and opened her mouth, spoke the words, "*Corpus Domini Nostri Iesu Christi custodiat animam tuam in vitam aeternam.*" Shirō understood some Latin. He had learned from Father Olivera, and even during his studies on Amakusa, where some of the Portuguese missionaries shared their knowledge of western medicine. Latin was so vastly different from Japanese, but Shirō had developed an appreciation for its precision and clarity. At any rate, he knew the meaning of the words the priest had just uttered: "May the Body of our Lord Jesus Christ preserve your soul to everlasting life." Father Olivera placed the small host into the waiting mouth of Shirō's mother just as a loud crash and the sound of splintered wood exploded into the small quiet space.

三

NIGHT MISSION
夜の使命

*"The angel of the Lord shall encamp round about them
that fear him, and shall deliver them."*
Psalm 34:7

"A single prayer moves heaven."
Japanese proverb

Everyone in the church spun their heads toward the explosive sound. A soldier in full dress armor appeared in the space where he had kicked the door open and off its now fractured frame. He entered and stood to one side of the gaping hole. Through the space emerged Lord Onizuka. He had to remove his helmet with its long horns in order to clear the entry. A line of soldiers filed in after him.

A hush fell over the space as all eyes were on the imposing form of the intruder. He said nothing but surveyed the room, taking in every face as if to make an inventory of them in his mind. The chiseled features of his own face were framed by a mane of dark hair, and he had a severe, penetrating stare that was frightful to behold yet irresistible. He reminded Shirō of one of the *koma-inu* lion-dog statues that guarded Kotahira Shrine on Shikoku Island. Onizuka continued scanning the room, like a predatory animal deciding which weak member of the flock might be the most opportune to devour.

Father Olivera broke the silence. "What is the meaning of this?" His voice was steady, though Shirō could detect a measure of apprehension.

None of the soldiers had removed their boots, and Lord Onizuka left a trail of mud upon the *tatami* floor as he walked brusquely toward Father Olivera, who was still holding the chalice filled with consecrated hosts. With one swift and powerful motion, Onizuka struck the priest with the back of his gloved fist. Father Olivera was sent reeling back hard against the altar behind him. The chalice flew from his hand, as the small hosts within it scattered across the floor. Shirō instinctively made a move to help his friend, but his father grabbed him firmly by the arm before he could step forward.

As if he had detected Shirō's intent, Lord Onizuka turned in his direction. He saw the look of anger on the boy's face and smiled. "I know there are warriors here among you. As a professional courtesy, you will all be permitted to leave here today. But upon the edict of Iemitsu Tokugawa himself, the practice of the foreign religion is hereby forbidden. No one is to enter nor come near this place. Likewise, the practice of any rituals, the possession of any images related to *Kirisuto*, or even uttering the very name, will result in grave consequences." Then, turning to his men, he ordered, "Take the priest away."

The soldiers seized a hold of Father Olivera, as droplets of blood from his mouth stained the *tatami* floor. They shoved him roughly toward the broken doorway while kicking and jeering at him. Then everyone was ordered to withdraw from the church. Outside, Father Olivera's hands were bound with a thick rope attached to the saddle horn of one of the soldiers. The villagers watched in silence as the intruders rode off, leaving but a thin cloud of dust behind them.

After a while, Shirō finally spoke. "What will we do, Otōsan?"

"I will go to Hitoyoshi Castle. I must learn if my Lord Yanazume is aware of what has happened."

Shirō replied, "I will go with you."

"*Iie.* I want you to go home and watch over your mother. I do not wish for her to be alone."

Shirō obediently answered, "*Hai, wakarimasu.*"

Shirō looked around in search of Kumiko, but she had already departed with her family. He then returned to his own home with his parents. His mother prepared some rice balls for her husband to take on his journey to the castle. Shirō watched his father as he shoved one of them whole into his mouth. Then Shirō said, "I did not receive the Blessed Sacrament."

"Not today," said his father. "But you shall."

Shirō's mind returned to the present as a human figure darted from the village toward the edge of the woods. The full moon reflected brightly upon the surface of the river and as Shirō focused his gaze, he could see that it was Kumiko. "What is she up to?" he whispered to himself. Without thinking, he followed her, maintaining sufficient distance to avoid being detected.

He reached the end of the path and came to the clearing

where the church stood. Despite the warning to stay away, there was no sign of any guard. He had also lost sight of Kumiko. Shirō waited at the edge of the wood, looking in all directions for some sign of her. Then, from behind a tree, her figure dashed across the clearing to one side of the church where there was a small open window. She stopped and turned to scan the perimeter of the clearing.

Shirō thought to himself, "What is she doing?" He could not imagine what cause she would have to return here after the events of that morning. With some effort, she hoisted herself onto the window's ledge and slid her lithe body through the opening. Shirō looked around but saw no sign of anyone else. As a cloud passed before the moon, he shot across the clearing to the window. He was tall enough to see through it, and he squinted as he peered into the dark church.

For several moments he could see nothing but the outlines of objects. But as his eyes adjusted, he detected movement. There was something moving slowly along the floor. At first he thought it was some animal, but he soon realized it was Kumiko. She was on her hands and knees upon the *tatami* floor. She moved slowly and methodically, as if looking for something. Then she lowered her head closer to the floor. She moved a little farther along, and repeated the action. "Is she looking for something she lost?" Shirō wondered if Kumiko had any possessions worth risking her life to retrieve. The thought of her doll came to mind, but he quickly dismissed it.

Shirō continued to observe as Kumiko crawled in the direction of the altar. As his eyes adjusted fully to the dim light filtering into the church, he finally saw what she was doing. As she moved along on all fours, she was consuming the consecrated Hosts directly from the floor.

A part of Shirō wanted to alert Kumiko to his presence. At the same time, he did not wish to startle her. As he pondered a gentle way of getting her attention, he saw movement from the gaping opening where the door had been smashed apart. So a guard had been posted there after all. He was a big oafish looking brute who lumbered as if he'd been drinking or just awoken from a nap, or both. Kumiko heard his heavy footfalls, and she reflexively spun around. The guard, realizing he'd allowed someone to enter under his watch, appeared more annoyed than surprised. He drew his sword and advanced upon Kumiko, as Shirō watched helplessly from the window. The guard raised his weapon to strike, but stopped once he was close enough to get a good look at the interloper.

"Well, what have we here?" With one of his pudgy hands, the guard reached down and roughly yanked Kumiko up off the floor by the lapel of her *kimono*. He leered at her as a wide grin traveled across his fat face. "Perhaps this *bakana* watch duty won't be a complete waste of my time." With the lapel still in his grip, he pulled down hard on the *kimono*. It tore and came open in the front. Then he pushed Kumiko back down onto the floor and leaned over her. With one hand, Kumiko pulled the long *kanzashi* stick from her hair. It was pointed at one end, and she drove it hard into the shoulder of her assailant. With a stunned expression, he grabbed the protruding object and yanked it out. He tossed it aside and struck Kumiko hard across the face.

Shirō, still standing at the window, felt himself filled with rage. He reached for his waist and realized he had left his own sword at home. He ran around the corner of the church to the broken doorway. Rushing in, he spied the wooden statue of Saint Michael and grabbed it with both hands. It was heavy, but he was able to wield it.

His back to Shirō, the guard was now on his knees and leaning over Kumiko. She tried to back away from him, but he grabbed her by the ankles and yanked her toward him. Shirō recalled the words of one of the fighting instructors from his youth. "Wherever the head goes, the body will follow." With one purposeful motion, Shirō swung the statue in a wide arc, striking it squarely upon the left temple of the guard. The man's entire body lifted from the *tatami* and spun around in mid-air. He landed on his back hard upon the communion rail. He shook his head as if to disperse the pain, and his eyes fixed upon Shirō. "You little runt!" he bellowed, bringing himself to his feet.

The guard raised his *katana* above his head and swung it straight down. Shirō, still firmly grasping the wooden statue, lifted it up to protect himself. The sword came down and embedded itself deep into the solid wood. The guard tried to pull the blade back, but Shirō twisted the statue sharply to one side, causing the hilt of the weapon to come loose from the guard's grip. The big man staggered back a few paces as Shirō tossed the statue, along with the blade, out of reach.

Now the guard, face flushed with fury, rushed upon Shirō at full force. Realizing he could not overpower the brute, Shirō braced himself for the impact.

Kumiko, witnessing the confrontation from the sanctuary, grabbed hold of the incense thurible with its long thick metal chain to which a weighty censer was attached. As the guard rushed at Shirō, she swung the thurible, in the manner of a ball-in-chain flail. The bronze censer hit the guard on the side of his head, in nearly the same swollen spot he'd been struck by Saint Michael. He halted his rush toward Shirō, and stood dazed as he held his hand up to his injury.

Kumiko, still holding the chain of the thurible, threw it around the fleshy neck of the guard, and yanked it as hard as she could. The guard's eyes bulged from their sockets, and he reached up to his throat.

With the guard's hands at his throat, his torso became an ample, unprotected target. Shirō ran forward and delivered a hard front kick to the man's sternum. The guard fell back and landed again upon the communion rail. Shirō immediately recognized the opportunity to flee, and he called out to Kumiko. But she seemed not to hear him. As Shirō stood and watched, Kumiko, now on her back and with her feet pressed against the rail, continued to pull the chain with all her might as it sank deeper into the guard's throat. The man struggled to free himself as his legs flailed like the tail of a gasping fish hoisted onto a boat. Shirō thought to intervene, but he stood frozen. Eventually, the flailing legs went limp and the big man's body lay still.

But for the sound of their breathing, there was silence for several moments before Shirō spoke. "Kumiko, are you alright?"

She looked at Shirō and there was confusion in her expression. "Where did you come from?"

"I followed you here from the village. Come, we must leave quickly."

Taking one another by the hand, the two ran out of the church and into the night.

四

Seeking Answers
答えを探す

*"No man can serve two masters. For either he will hate
the one, and love the other, or he will sustain the one,
and despise the other."*
Matthew 6:24

*"The true meaning of the samurai is one who serves and
adheres to the power of love."*
Morihei Ueshiba

It was dark when they reached the main gate of the castle. Earlier that evening, Hiromu had looked all around his home and the village for Shirō, but he was nowhere to be found. Not wanting to leave his wife alone after the events of that morning, Hiromu decided to take Michiko with him to the castle. There he hoped to find some answers from his Lord Yanazume about what had transpired.

Hitoyoshi Castle rose up like a white sentinel on the eastern side of the Kuma River. Its long reflection danced upon the shimmering water under the bright light of the full moon. Like many castles, it much resembled a Chinese pagoda. Its five tiers symbolized each of the great elements

33

of earth, water, fire, wind and "the void." The steep roof lines of each level pointed upward like hands pressed together in prayerful supplication. The whole structure rested firmly atop a steep rock wall, named for its primary purpose, *musha-gaeshi*, "repelling warriors."

Hiromu was escorted by a servant up a steep stairwell to a small room where Lord Yanazume was seated upon a *zabuton* cushion before a low long table. Open before him was a book from which he was reading with rapt attention.

"My lord, please forgive this unannounced visit."

"*Iie, iie.*" Yanazume waved his hand in front of his own face to deflect the unnecessary apology. "Everything I touch with tenderness, alas, pricks like a bramble."

"My lord, excuse me? What was that?"

Yanazume laughed. "It's a poem from this book my wife has given me. It's a new style called *hokku*. They're short and meant to get straight to the point. What do you think?"

Hiromu was not a great lover of poetry, but he replied, "I admit it does convey a sentiment most commonly experienced."

"Yes, yes, indeed it does. What do you think of this one?" Yanazume recited, "Lightning flash—what I thought were faces, are plumes of pampas grass."

"I can certainly picture the image in my mind."

"Ah! That is the whole idea."

Kashigi Yanazume was smaller in stature than Hiromu, though equally stout and thicker around the waist. His impeccable posture made him appear larger and gave him an air of great confidence. He had the shaved top of the head, common amongst the *samurai* class, but thick sideburns and a thin moustache. A shiny scar, from a long-healed wound, ran down his cheek from the corner of his left eye.

Hiromu had been in Yanazume's service as long as any

other *samurai*, and the two men had forged a mutual respect and strong friendship over the years. There had been many a discussion between them, often lasting deep into the evening—about politics and philosophy, warfare and women, and more recently, the many facets of *Kirisutokyō*, from its strangest mysteries to its everyday applications.

"I apologize also for bringing my wife. There is much amiss in the village. Our son was not at hand, and I did not wish to leave her alone." Upon their arrival at the castle, Hiromu and Michiko had been greeted by Lady Yanazume, who took Michiko aside and to her private chamber.

"Again, no need for apologies. My wife will be glad for the company." Lord Yanazume rang a small bell, and a door panel slid open. A young female attendant entered, her head down and her hands at the neatly tied *obi* around her waist, the fingers of her right hand perfectly overlapping those of her left. "*O-cha*," Yanazume directed with the word for "tea."

"*Hai, Yanazume-sama.*" The attendant pivoted flawlessly and walked back toward the open door.

Yanazume called to her before she exited, "And bring *shōchū!*"

The attendant gave a gentle nod and smiled as she exited the room, sliding the door shut silently behind her. Yanazume turned back toward Hiromu. "You say there is something amiss in the village?"

"My lord, this morning's *Misa* was violated by a platoon from Yatsushiro. They took Shinpu and declared that The Way is no longer to be practiced."

Lord Yanazume looked down and let out a heavy sigh. "Old friend, there has been much happening in Kyōto. It has only taken a while to reach us here."

"What exactly is going on, my lord?"

"Hidetada Tokugawa's son, Iemistsu, has been formally

named as the new *shōgun*."

Hiromu was about to say that this came as little surprise to him. It was well known that the elder Tokugawa was advancing in age and failing in health. Iemitsu controlled much of the internal politics from behind the scenes. The transfer of the title was merely an eventual inevitability, especially considering Hidetada's daughter, Masako, was the wife of the recently abdicated emperor, Go-Mizunō.

Now the reigning monarch was the emperor's teenage daughter, the empress Meishō, only the seventh woman in the history of the empire to sit upon the chrysanthemum throne. And if Go-Mizunō had been a political puppet to his father-in-law, how much more would that prove to be true of Meishō, young niece of the newly installed *shōgun*?

Hiromu, not wishing to interrupt his master, continued to listen.

"I had long prayed for the emperor," continued Yanazume. "I prayed that he might find the fortitude and the strength to truly rule once again, rather than yield his natural authority to amoral men of ambition. Moreover, I fervently prayed for his conversion. I truly believed that his baptism would be the single greatest event in the history of our people. Had the living heir of Amaterasu proclaimed the primacy of the one triune God, he could have consecrated all his subjects to Our Blessed Lord. But given the new *shōgun*'s disdain for the Christian missionaries and converts, I can see no way this will happen."

"Still, we must continue to pray for the conversion of souls," Hiromu finally spoke when he sensed a natural space. "I understand the young empress has expressed some degree of curiosity about The Way."

Yanazume uttered a grunt of resignation. "There is no chance that her grandfather, Hidetada, nor her uncle,

Iemistsu, would allow the empress to even look upon a baptismal font. For them, anything from the outside world is to be regarded with suspicion if not contempt."

"They certainly embraced the Portuguese *arquebus* with open arms."

"Yes, well, firearms are always the exception, aren't they? The Tokugawas are certainly pragmatic when it comes to temporal affairs. But I fear it was some of our own who helped bring about the present dilemma."

"How do you mean?"

"One of the Christian *daimyō*, Lord Arima, bribed a government official, also one of the baptized, to reclaim land he had lost to a rival during the time of the Sengoku wars. In order to grant the request, the official had to forge documents bearing the royal seal. Their scheme was discovered, and the official was put to death by the *mino odori*.* Arima was ordered to commit *seppuku*, but he refused, stating our belief that to take one's own life is a mortal sin. So, the younger Tokugawa had him beheaded. This incident gave the authorities just the reason needed to point to followers of The Way, and label them as criminals and cowards. The sins of our brethren bring shame and consequences upon us all."

The attendant returned with a tray carrying two ceramic cups and a container filled with the heated *shōchū*. She filled each of the cups nearly to its brim. Lord Yanazume held his cup aloft, uttered the obligatory, "*Kampai!*" and downed the slightly bitter beverage. Hiromu placed his cup to his lips but did not drink, instead placing the full cup back down onto the tray before them. Yanazume eyed the cup and said, "I see you are still abstaining?"

---

*Literally, "raincoat dance," a form of execution by which one was adorned with a coat of straw, doused in oil, and set alight.

"It just doesn't seem to agree with me. *Sumimasen.*" Hiromu had not taken any *shōchū*, nor even *sake*, its weaker cousin, in nearly two years. In his younger days he had partaken all too frequently, most often in the company of comrades. Not long after the first few sips, most of them would exhibit the telltale flushing of the face, along with the general feeling of euphoria. But Hiromu was rarely able to leave it at that. He would nearly always continue to the point of intoxication, which would be followed by the agony of the next morning's *futsukayoi*, and even blackouts of memory from the previous night.

He would often return home in a stupor late in the night, acting sullen, even hostile. There were frequent rows with Michiko, and for a long while their relationship became estranged. One night, when Hiromu came home in a particularly bad state, he flailed about the house, raising his voice in anger about how untidy the place was (when in truth this was hardly the case). This then led into a tirade about how nothing in his life was the way he intended it to be. Young Shirō, only four at the time, stood crying in a doorway. He pointed an accusing finger at Hiromu and shouted, "Who are you? You are not my papa! My papa would not say such things! What have you done to my papa?"

With those words, something in Hiromu was shaken. After that night, he avoided the occasions where the "wicked water" might be present. After his conversion, he made the decision to abstain altogether during the penitential season preceding the high celebration of the Passion and Resurrection. During this time, he enjoyed a feeling of clarity and well being he hadn't felt in a very long time. His relationship with his wife also underwent a reconciliation.

"Well," said Yanazume, "then I suppose there will be more for me!" With that, he downed another cup of *shōchū*, and motioned to the attendant to pour Hiromu some tea. She did so and then quietly took her leave. Yanazume continued with his tale.

"Hundreds of the faithful attended Arima's funeral. They paid their respects and prayed for the salvation of his soul. This infuriated the younger Tokugawa. That was the point at which he decided to put an end to it. He wrote this proclamation and had it sent to all the *daimyō*." Yanazume picked up a small scroll next to his poetry book on the table and read,

> *"When the Christians see a condemned fellow,*
> *they run to him with joy,*
> *bow to him, and do him reverence.*
> *This they say is the essence of their belief.*
> *If this is not an evil law, what is it?*
> *They truly are the enemies of the gods and of Buddha."*

Hiromu was listening intently. He had met Arima on his most recent visit to Kyōto. They had even attended *Misa* there together. "How were Arima and the official found out, my Lord?"

"Arima's son reported him directly to the younger Tokugawa."

"His own son?"

"Yes, his eldest son, Naozumi. Like his father, Naozumi had been baptized and taken a Christian wife. But in the reporting of his father's crime, he saw an opportunity to gain favor with the elder Tokugawa. And, indeed, he did. After the executions, Tokugawa offered one of his concubinal granddaughters to Naozumi in marriage. Perhaps this was a test to see where Naozumi's allegiance lay. Naozumi rejected the faith and his legitimate bride to take the new wife and demonstrate his loyalty to Tokugawa."

Hiromu absorbed all of this for a few moments and shook his head. "A man cannot serve two masters."

"Yes, the truth of these words we have known even before we heard them spoken by Iesu. But Naozumi's devotion to his new master is quite singular. The younger Tokugawa sent Naozumi to Yatsushiro with the mission of shutting down all churches in Kyūshū. To demonstrate his resolve, he even put to death, by his own sword, his two Christian half-brothers. They were eight and six years old."

Hiromu cast his eyes downward. He had witnessed much brutality in his lifetime, but the execution of innocents was something he could not stomach.

"In the meantime, Iemitsu Tokugawa has ordered that all priests and missionaries be expelled. Any attempt to return will be punishable by death. And I have learned that this has already happened. A Portuguese ship arriving in Nagasaki from Macau was found to have two priests on board. They were dressed as laymen, but a search of the ship revealed their vestments. Not only the priests, but even the captain and crew were put to death. One of those priests was my first confessor."

Hiromu saw that his master's cup was empty. He took the ceramic bottle and filled the cup with more of the *shōchū*. It was still warm.

"The peasants are now bearing the brunt of young Tokugawa's ire," Yanazume continued. "The Christian villages are being taxed even more heavily than before. There is now a birth tax for every newborn child, and a hole tax for those burying the bodies of believers. Even simple household items such as shelves and windows are to be taxed. Those unable to procure the required portion of rice are imprisoned. There have already been reports of beatings of peasants and abuse of women."

"My lord, you said the son of Arima, Naozumi, was sent by Tokugawa to Yatsushiro Castle. The men who broke into the church today bore banners from Yatsushiro."

"To further distance himself from the shame of his criminal Christian father, Naozumi disowned his own family name, and took that of his new bride, Tokugawa's granddaughter. He took for himself the name of Onizuka."

"My lord, all that you have spoken troubles me deeply. In the face of such a turning of the tide, what are we to do?"

"For the moment, my faithful friend, nothing."

五.

An Old Friend Returns
昔の友達が帰って来る

*"A friend loves at all times, and a brother is born
for a time of adversity."*
Proverbs 17:17

*"A real friend is one who walks in when the rest of the
world walks out."*
Japanese proverb

"But we must do something. We cannot simply let them take Shinpu away." Kumiko spoke softly, yet her words conveyed the weightiness of command.

"Yes, I know," replied Shirō. "But I fear there is nothing we can do right at this moment." He called out for his mother, but there was no answer. He turned back to Kumiko, "Come, sit down. I will bring you some tea. Are you sure you're alright?"

Kumiko answered, her eyes cast down toward the floor. *"Hai, daijōbu."*

Shirō brought two ceramic cups and a pot of tea that his mother had brewed that morning. Beside the pot was a note.

43

He recognized his father's handwriting.

*"Shirō-kun, I am going with your mother to the castle.
I could not find you, and did not wish to leave her alone.
Stay and mind the house."*

The note was signed with the character for "father." 父

Shirō felt a fluttering sensation in his stomach. It was much like the one he felt his first night in Amakusa, the first night he had ever slept away from home. The fluttering had been accompanied by a dull ache of loneliness and a longing to be in the presence of his family. What had made these feelings worse was a belief that he could not admit them to anyone, for fear they were somehow inconsistent with manhood.

He turned back to Kumiko and poured some tea into her cup. It was tepid and bitter from having steeped the entire day. "Kumiko, going back to the church was very foolish. Why did you risk such a thing?"

"Our Blessed Lord was lying upon the floor. I could not simply leave Him there."

"But, Kumiko, that guard meant to do you harm. He might have killed you." Even as he spoke the words, the reality that they had been the ones to take a life began to sink in.

"If the body of someone you loved fell upon the field of battle, would you not risk your own skin to retrieve it? Would you not venture even into an enemy's camp to preserve the dignity of the body of your beloved?"

These questions caught Shirō off guard. They made him realize that, while the true presence of the Eucharist was something he had come to accept intellectually, Kumiko understood it in the depths of her heart. "I, I should like to think so, but..."

Shirō's answer was interrupted by the clack of hooves just outside the house. He ran to the adjoining room and grabbed his swords. "Kumiko, stay down!" Keeping low, Shirō made his way to the door and slid it open just enough to peer out. The first rays of dawn were just beginning to peek out over the line of hills. He saw a large horse of a light gray color, spotted with several darker patches. And mounted upon the steed was a figure that looked somehow familiar. A longbow and a quiver of arrows were strapped across the rider's back.

"Shirō-kun!" The rider yelled toward the house. "Shirō Nakagawa! Where are you? Show yourself, you scrawny scoundrel!"

Shirō squinted to better see. He knew that voice. The rider dismounted deftly from his horse and landed solidly onto the ground. He began to walk toward the house, and it was by his unmistakable gait that recognition in Shirō fully registered. He spoke aloud, "Tomi-kun!"

Tomi Ishibara had been Shirō's best friend from childhood. Three years Shirō's senior, he had been something of an older brother figure as they were growing up. Tomi had a big heart, but had always been at odds with the world. In particular, he had a sharp dislike for authority, starting with his own father. At the age of fifteen, he had a terrible row with his father who told him, "If you cannot abide the rules of my house, go make yourself a nest elsewhere!" And so Tomi did.

He left the village with nothing but the clothes on his back and a small sack filled with millet dumplings his weeping mother had made for his journey. Shirō had not seen nor heard from Tomi since the cherry blossoms were in bloom four years prior. He was unlike anyone else Shirō had ever known. Even his name was unusual. It was comprised of the characters for "jump over" and "ocean," so that it seemed fitting he should travel to someplace far from home.

He was as stocky as Shirō remembered, but now even broader in the shoulders. His hair was cropped close, just as it had been when they last saw one another. The ruggedness of his face, accentuated by a muscular neck and strong jaw, could not conceal a kindness in his almond shaped eyes that Shirō could perceive even from a distance. He ran out to greet his old friend.

Shirō recalled the time from their youth when a village bully and a gang of his companions took cruel pleasure in teasing Shirō on account of his family's newly adopted religion. It was the same gang of ruffians who had taken Kumiko's doll some years earlier. One hot afternoon by the river's edge, they taunted Shirō with particular ruthlessness. One of them shouted, "Your father worships a dead man nailed to a cross!"

Another one of them added, "Do you believe a god baby came from a virgin? You're a virgin, Shirō. Perhaps a baby will come out of you!"

Then the leader chimed in, "What did your looney Obāsan used to call you? Masaru? What did she reckon you would have victory over? Why don't you test your pet name on me, Masaru-chan!"

Shirō cared little to be mocked, but it was the flagrant disrespect toward the dead that caused anger to well up in him. And the anger grew larger than his fear. As he turned to face his tormentors, the leader gave Shirō a hard shove.

Shirō instinctively pushed back. The bigger and stronger bully slapped Shirō hard across the face and pushed him down onto the rocky ground. He then pounced on Shirō and raised up a fist to strike him in the face. Shirō could only wince as the bright sun behind his attacker shone brightly into his eyes.

The fist came down. But before it could make contact, another hand caught it by the wrist. It was Tomi, who seemed to have appeared from out of nowhere. Taken aback, the bully snapped his head toward Tomi. "Get out of here, Ishibara! This doesn't concern you."

"Yes, it does," replied Tomi in a tone that conveyed not so much defiance as correction. "This is my friend, and I don't like when a cockroach picks on a smaller bug to make himself feel big."

The bully stood to face Tomi, who was about his equal in size. "The only cockroach is this little bug's father. He worships a dead man, and believes in bread that turns into human flesh."

"Yes, well," replied Tomi, "at least he knows who his father is."

Anger flashed in the bully's eyes as he clenched his fists.

"Think twice before you do," said Tomi. "I promise you one thing. You start with me and one of us is leaving here with a broken face."

Realizing that Tomi was in earnest, the bully lowered his hands and turned to walk away. But, seeing the expressions on the faces of his comrades, pride got the better of him. He whirled back around to deliver a roundhouse punch to Tomi's left cheek. Rather than back away from the punch, Tomi stepped in toward his assailant and, with one fluid motion, slid his left leg behind the legs of the bully.

With the distance between them closed, the bully's

punch grazed harmlessly against Tomi's left shoulder. He then drove that same shoulder into the chest of the bully, sending him tumbling backwards over Tomi's solidly planted left leg. Without hesitation, Tomi dropped his left knee onto the bully's chest, pinning him to the ground. Tomi brought up his right hand and brought the heel of his palm straight down into the bully's nose. Shirō cringed as he heard the crunching of cartilage. He had never before seen so much blood.

Those boys never bothered Shirō again.

As they walked away from the river, Shirō said to Tomi, "That was quite a move you used back there. Where did you learn it?"

"Oh, I've been doing some training—and lots of reading."

"Reading?"

"*Hai*. Master Musashi has written a new book, *Go Rin No Sho*, The Book of Five Rings. You must read it. It's some excellent philosophy. I know you like to talk philosophy with your priest friend, but this is the kind that has practical use—not like your Christian 'love thy enemy' drivel. Give me the kind of philosophy that can help me subdue or trample my enemies!"

From that day, Shirō and Tomi spent many afternoons training together.

That was not the only time Tomi had come to Shirō's rescue. One year before Tomi's abrupt departure from the village, the two friends had been walking in the forest between Watari and the northern neighboring village of Takazawa. At one point, they became separated for a while, and Shirō figured Tomi was up to one of his usual ambush games. Hearing a rustling from some nearby underbrush, Shirō laughed and said, "Alright, Tomi-kun, you'll have to do better than that!"

Without warning, something low but large darted out from the brush. Shirō instinctively jumped to one side as one of the boar's tusks, which surely would have gored his thigh, instead grazed the outside of his leg. Shirō ran but soon found himself pinned against the steep hillside. The animal appeared agitated as it spun itself around, its big thick head cocked to one side. Shirō remained still in the hope that the brute would not see him. But its beady eyes fixed on Shirō as it once again charged. Shirō tried to judge whether he should dart to the left or right, but realized it would not much matter, given the size of the beast and the speed with which it was bearing down upon him.

As suddenly as the boar had sprung from the brush, it slumped over in a heap only a short distance from where Shirō stood frozen. When he opened his eyes, he saw that the massive thing lay still on its side, its bristly hide expanding and contracting like a swordmaker's bellows. Protruding from the base of its neck, just below the thick skull, was the shaft of an arrow. Shirō looked all around but could see no one. Then he heard a voice coming from above. "Hey, down there!" Shirō looked up and saw Tomi standing atop a high ledge, the sun bright behind him. "I was going to ambush you, but I see someone beat me to it!"

After ensuring that the beast was lifeless, the two friends took several hours, right up to nightfall, to drag its great weight back to the village, where *shishi-nabe* and other pork dishes were enjoyed for the next several days.

"Tomi, I can't tell you how good it is to see you." Shirō smiled and clasped the shoulders of his returned companion. "I must believe God brought you here precisely when I needed to see a familiar face."

"My, you've sprouted like a weed!" Indeed, since the time they had last seen one another, Shirō had gone from one head shorter to one head taller than Tomi. "You know I don't believe in gods, Shirō. But perhaps, in a way, you may be right that it was your God who brought me here. Come, let us go inside. I am weary from travel."

Back inside the house, the three sat around the single low table and sipped the bitter tea that still filled the pot. "Tomi-kun," Shirō began, "Where have you been all this time?"

"In Nagasaki, mostly. I found work in the port. The arriving Spanish and Portuguese ships needed hands to help them unload their cargo. It paid well enough for me to keep my belly fed, my head rested, and my body bathed. I haven't need of much else."

"You remember Kumiko-chan?"

Tomi examined the pretty young woman sitting across from him, scanning for something familiar. He found it as he looked into her round chestnut eyes. "Ah, yes. Shimamura-san. I remember when you were just a little *chibikko* ankle biter playing in the paddies! You've certainly grown up." Kumiko smiled and cast her eyes down.

Shirō was quick to interrupt. "You chose an interesting time to come home, Tomi-kun. Much has been happening here."

Tomi nodded, his face becoming grave. "Much is happening everywhere."

"What do you mean?" Kumiko posed the question.

"Back in Nagasaki, they executed twenty-six men. Well, I should say twenty-three men. The other three were only boys, the youngest only twelve. They were some of your fellow Christians. Six of them were *gaijin*, including three priests, but the other twenty were our own people, including the young ones. They were hoisted up on crosses, much like that one you wear around your neck, Shirō." Tomi pointed to the wooden cross at Shirō's chest, secured by a slender cord of leather. It was from Portugal and had been a baptismal gift from Father Olivera. "Yes, they were hoisted up on crosses, and then run through with spears."

Shirō's eyes widened. "When did this happen?"

"Less than a week ago. I saw them marched into the city and up to Nishizaka Hill. A thin coat of snow had just fallen. They were forced to march all the way from Kansai where they were arrested. Apparently they refused to renounce your beloved Savior. And so they were made to walk the long distance, passing through every town and village to serve as an example. At some point along the way, their left ears were hacked off, supposedly to show what would happen to others who attempted to hear or proclaim this—what do you call it? —Gospel of yours."

"You say you saw this happen?" asked Kumiko.

"Yes, as did many others. We stood alongside the road as they marched past. I could literally see the drops of blood that fell from their heads onto the snow. I followed behind them up to the hilltop. I'm not sure why, but I could not stop myself. There were wooden crosses, lying on the ground, waiting for each of them. The captives were tied to the crosses and then raised up for all to see. Soldiers with spears were stationed on either side of the condemned ones. When the order was given, the spears were run straight through their bodies in the shape of an X—in through the rib cage, and out through the back of the neck. The deaths were not quick."

Kumiko hastily gathered the empty cups onto a tray, and carried it toward the hearth, saying, "I shall prepare a fresh pot of tea."

"I shouldn't have spoken of this in front of her," Tomi said quietly, leaning in toward Shirō. "I'm afraid my travels didn't teach me much tact."

"It's alright," said Shirō. "She's been through quite a lot in the past two days. We both have."

"Where is your family, by the way?"

"My parents have gone to Hitoyoshi. Obāsan passed away a little over two years ago."

"I am sorry to hear that. I very much enjoyed the talks I had with her. She was quite a feisty lady!"

"*Hai,* that she was. And she was always quite fond of you, but for reasons I could never quite understand! But please continue your story."

"I stood there and watched until the soldiers ordered us to disperse. Some of the people were beginning to pray, but the soldiers would have none of it. They pulled a few peasants aside and gave them a pretty sound beating. I went back to my room at the inn, though I hadn't much stomach for food. I did go to the bath house, but could not wash the images from my mind. Later that night, I returned to the foot of the hill. I saw the silhouette of those twenty-six crosses, each with its X of spears. For a moment, I didn't even give a thought to those poor souls, impaled and hanging there. I simply gazed and marvelled at the symmetry of the scene. Is that not an odd thing?"

Shirō was silent for a while. Finally he said, "Last night, we killed a soldier from Yatsushiro."

Tomi turned to face Shirō, and raised an eyebrow. After a long silence, he finally said, "I see. Well, I hope the poor fellow at least deserved it!" Shirō then had his turn to share with Tomi all the events since the previous morning, after which Tomi declared, "Yes, well, I'd say, based on all you've said, the brute indeed deserved it. There was a man I wanted to kill on my way here from Nagasaki, though I was not afforded the opportunity."

Kumiko returned to the table with a fresh pot of tea. "Tell us."

"Three nights ago, I arrived in Kōnose village as the sun was beginning to set. One of the farmers there was gracious enough to put me up for the night. It was a Christian family—the man, his wife, and three young daughters. I had to bear their little rituals, you know, the prayers before meals, evening and morning prayers, lots of prayers. You Christians are as bad as the Buddhists when it comes to all your prayers! But, of course, I couldn't complain. They treated me very kindly—fed me well, drew me a bath, even allowed me to sleep indoors amongst them.

The next morning, as we sat down to breakfast, men rode into the village from across the river. I could tell from their banners they were from Yatsushiro Castle. They ordered everyone outside and into the common area by the *torī* gate. The villagers had no idea why these men had arrived, but I had some clue. I had not told the family about what I'd witnessed in Nagasaki."

"The soldiers corralled the people around the *torī* gate," Tomi continued. "Then the leader, a tall man wearing the *kabuto* helmet, held up a *fumie*, a bronze image of your Iesu upon the cross. He told the people they must tread upon it and renounce the Christian God. There was much agitation among the people, and they began to protest. The *kabuto* became impatient. He threw the bronze image onto the ground, and grabbed an old man standing beside me. He was ordered to step with his foot upon the image, but the old man protested. The *kabuto* unsheathed his sword and asked the old man whether it was worth losing his head over the image of a man who was already dead. I could smell the fear coming off the poor fellow. He finally stepped on the image and knelt down weeping at the edge of the crowd."

Kumiko asked, "You say the leader wore the *kabuto*?"

"*Hai.*"

Kumiko and Shirō looked at one another.

Tomi asked, "Is he the one you killed?"

"No," said Shirō. "But he may have been the one who broke into the church yesterday. Please go on."

"Well, the *kabuto* seemed pretty pleased with himself, having gotten the first poor fool he grabbed to step on the image. He then gave the order that everyone in the village, even the children, must do the same. Some big brute of a fellow grabbed me and told me to step on it."

"And did you?" asked Kumiko.

"Not at first."

"What made you hesitate?" asked Kumiko. "Was there something in your heart telling you there was perhaps more to the image than mere bronze?"

Tomi laughed. "No, Shimamura-san, I'm afraid that wasn't it at all. I don't believe what you believe. I just don't take kindly to being told what to do, and I gave the soldier a look to let him know it. Then he gave me a punch to the gut to let me know he didn't like the look I gave him. But, yes, I stepped on the thing so that I could walk away from there. But before I walked away, I stayed around long enough to see the farmer, my host from that night, forced to take his turn to step on the image. He wouldn't do it. They slapped him around pretty good, but he still wouldn't just step on the damned thing."

"So what happened?" asked Kumiko.

Tomi fidgeted with his empty cup. "They grabbed a hold of his oldest daughter. She was about your age. They tore off her clothes and commanded the farmer to step on the image. The poor fellow began to sob, but he still wouldn't do it. He begged them to leave her alone. They just laughed. Then the big brute who struck me took a pair of tongs and held the bronze piece over the charcoals of a cooking fire. Once it was good and hot, he pressed it against the girl's thigh, right below her buttocks. She cried out in agony while the family was made to watch. The father was out of his mind. Now the image upon which he refused to tread is forever branded in the flesh of his child."

No one spoke for a while. Finally, Tomi said, "I can't understand. Why didn't the poor fool just step on the damned thing? Did he believe this Iesu of yours would have punished him for it? Even to save his own daughter from disgrace and disfigurement? Wouldn't you have stepped on it?"

Shirō answered, "I don't know, Tomi-san."

The three of them were silent for a while longer. Finally, Shirō looked up at Tomi. "Old friend," he said, "will you help me to help another friend?"

六

TO SAVE A PRIEST
司祭を救う

*"Who covereth the heaven with clouds, and prepareth
rain for the earth. Who maketh grass to grow on the
mountains, and herbs for the service of men."*
Psalm 147:8

*"The clouds come and go, providing a rest for all the
moon viewers."*
Matsuo Bashō

"My lord, we found Goto in the church. He is dead."
There was tension in the soldier's voice and shoulders.
"It appears he was drunk and hit his head."

"I see." Lord Onizuka mounted his horse as he prepared
to lead his men back to Yatsushiro Castle.

"Shall we bring his body with us for the proper rites?"

"*Iie.* Burn the church with his body in it. That will suffice
for his funeral."

"*Hai, Tono!* And the prisoner? Shall we mount him onto
one of the horses?"

"Our beasts will not bear the backside of that foreign
filth. He will go to Yatsushiro on his own two feet." Onizuka

57

motioned to two of his soldiers, already seated upon their horses. "You two! Stay and torch the church. Let the priest see it burn to the ground. Then bring him back to the castle. The rest of us are riding ahead. Let him suffer the entire walk, but I want him to arrive alive. Do you understand?"

In unison, they responded affirmatively, "*Hai*, Onizuka-sama! *Wakarimashita!*"

Father Olivera's throat was parched from thirst. He'd been given no water by his captors. His wrists were chafed by the rough rope that bound his hands tightly together. As he spied the sun coming up above the treeline, he made a sign of the cross and offered up his customary morning prayer.

> *"My God, I love thee above all things, with my whole heart and soul, because thou art all good and worthy of all love. I love my neighbor as myself for the love of thee. I forgive all who have injured me, and ask pardon of all whom I have injured."*

The larger of the two soldiers assigned to guard him came over and gave him a kick. "On your feet, priest. You have a long walk ahead."

Olivera knew the distance to Yatsushiro to be about thirteen *ri*. He had walked such distances on many occasions, but it would be difficult in his current condition. In addition to buffeting him with kicks and punches, the soldiers had also stripped him of his sandals. The smaller of the guards came and tied a longer rope to the one binding Olivera's hands. The other end of the rope was fastened to the horn of a horse's saddle. The guards mounted, and the long march was underway.

"Jump in," said Shirō. "We're borrowing old man Tanaka's boat."

"You think he's going to mind?" asked Tomi, even as he climbed aboard and laid his bow next to Shirō's sword on the bottom boards of the small fishing boat.

"He hurt his back a week ago. I don't think he'll be needing it for a while. Anyway, we'll return it to him."

After Shirō had told Tomi the story of Father Olivera's capture, Tomi recalled that he had seen a priest back at Kōnose village. While the villagers were being made to tread upon the *fumie*, Tomi saw a foreigner, wearing priest's vestments, being led by guards to a small hut. But that had been three days ago, so it could not have been Father Olivera.

After some discussion, it was decided that Kumiko should return to her family home with Tomi's horse. (She knew her younger brothers would be excited to help care for the animal.) Shirō and Tomi realized that the best chance to liberate Father Olivera would be to get ahead of him and his captors by way of the river, which was flowing free and fast.

Growing up, the two friends had occasionally taken a boat down the river, one time even as far as Sakamoto village, nearly halfway to Yatsushiro where the river emptied into the bay. Inside old man Tanaka's boat was some fishing gear, as well as two wide-brimmed cone-shaped hats which they decided to leave in the boat. Shirō untied the rope that secured the boat to a nearby post, pushed off into the current, and jumped in alongside Tomi.

It was turning out to be a nearly perfect late autumn day. The sun was directly overhead, but a steady breeze carried the chill from the water's surface into the air. The brilliant colors of the fall foliage were at their peak. The woods along the river's banks and covering the hillsides were painted with the crimson of maples, wax trees, rowan, burning bush, and sumac, while linden, ginkgo, elms, and poplars exploded with clusters of golden highlights. Even the browns of the birches, chestnuts, oaks, and beeches provided a contrast that made the other colors appear all the more brilliant.

Shirō took hold of the tiller to keep the boat in the river's center and away from the many outcroppings of rock. For a while, the two friends were transported further back to their youth, to a time when such excursions in nature were many, and worldly cares were few. Shirō lifted his face up to the sky as the warm sun and cool mist kissed his senses. He gazed upon the thick cottony clouds as they passed overhead. They reminded him of great land masses like the ones on the Portuguese maps he had seen in Amakusa. He imagined that the cloud continents were populated with cities and villages, and that perhaps the people in them were looking up and seeing his world as merely one of their passing clouds.

"They are quite beautiful, aren't they?" said Tomi. For a fleeting instant, Shirō thought Tomi was talking about the people in his vision, but quickly realized that he was of course talking about the clouds themselves.

"Yes, they are," answered Shirō. Then, after a few moments he asked, "Did you ever wonder why?"

"Why what?" asked Tomi.

"Why they are beautiful."

"What do you mean?"

"I mean, why is it that we find clouds to be beautiful?

After all, they're little more than masses of condensed water vapor."

"Yes, well, I suppose there's something about them that captures the imagination. Just the sheer variety of their shape and texture. Not even a week ago, I observed a thick blanket of those clouds that look like the scales of a giant fish or dragon. You know the kind I mean. The setting sun illuminated them in such a way as to make them appear like the *obon* lanterns as they float along the river."

"Oh, I agree," offered Shirō. "But what I find fascinating is that there is, at least as far as I can ascertain, no reason why it needs to be so."

Tomi raised an eyebrow. "I don't understand what you mean."

"I suppose what I mean is that clouds, like so many things, serve a necessary purpose. They collect and transport life-giving water across the earth, and for that alone we can be most grateful. And yet they possess a beauty that leads me to believe that they exist for us to behold with wonder and pleasure. It's as though, as with the colors of autumn and so many of nature's intricacies, they were created to give delight to creatures endowed with a capacity to contemplate beauty. It is as though they were fashioned by one who is not only a master designer, but also a sublime artist."

Tomi seemed to consider this for a while. Finally he said, "Shirō, I thought you were strange when we were kids. I think you're even stranger now."

Shirō laughed and the two continued to enjoy the glorious autumn sky a while longer.

After some time had passed, Tomi spoke again, "Are you sure you want to risk this, Shirō? You do realize they may kill us, yes?"

"*Hai.* I do understand. I know the soldier in the church

would have killed me. I saw it in his eyes. I believe he might have killed Kumiko as well, after having his way with her. Tomi-san, if you can't help me, I understand. I would not hold it against you."

Tomi laughed. "Well, what a fine time to tell me that—when I'm already in the boat!" He paused for a moment and his face became serious again. "I just don't know why you need to risk such a thing. I know he's your friend, but he's not even one of us. It is possible they won't kill him. I've heard most of the priests are being sent back to Spain and Portugal. The ones I saw executed may have just been exceptions."

"That's not very reassuring. And anyway, this is his homeland now, Tomi. Just as much as it is yours and mine."

"I know he's been here a long time, Shirō, but his blood is not the same as ours."

"Is it not, Tomi? Is it truly not the same?"

Tomi was about to answer but then looked past Shirō as something along the shore caught his eye. "Shirō, there they are!" Shirō turned around and saw on the western shore the sight of two riders on horseback. About ten paces behind the rear horse was another man, naked from the waist up, his hands held up in front of him. "Quickly," said Tomi, "put on the hats."

The men on horse spied the boat and watched as it went by. Shirō and Tomi busied themselves appearing to be engaged in the activity of fishing and navigation. They paused, however, to acknowledge and bow to the figures on land as the boat floated past. The figures returned the gesture with a simple nod of their heads. Once they had floated far enough for the figures on land to become small dots, they removed the hats. Tomi asked, "Alright, Shirō. What now?"

"The Shibatate shrine is just up ahead. They will stop there to get fresh water." It was well known to those in the region that the shrine had been erected near a natural spring. The builders of the shrine had also fashioned a ceramic fountain from which visitors could draw the perpetually flowing water for drinking or washing.

The two friends put the boat into shore and hid it in the brush and weeds beneath a rock outcropping. They gathered their weapons and were about to make haste toward the shrine. Shirō, spying some large pieces of cloth in the boat, said, "Let's take these as well."

"Alright, priest, we're stopping here." The smaller guard dismounted the horse to which the priest was bound and tethered it to a short post beside the shrine. A wooden platform ran along the ground from the post in one direction to the entrance of the shrine. In the opposite direction, the platform extended to the fountain. The larger guard took a small wooden cup with a long handle beside the fountain, and filled it with water. He gulped it down, the cool water running down both sides of his face. Then he filled the cup again and drank some more. He rinsed the cup and handed it to his comrade, who also drank his fill. The smaller guard was about to hand the cup to the prisoner, but before it reached the priest's bound hands, the larger man knocked the cup away.

"No, you drink straight from the fountain. I don't want your lips touching my cup!" The two guards mocked Father Olivera as he knelt down to drink. Oblivious to their ridicule, he lowered his mouth and lapped like a dog at the cool stream.

The guards' amusement was short lived, and the smaller one shouted, "Alright, you've had enough." But Olivera kept drinking, knowing this might be his last chance to take water for a very long time. The smaller guard advanced toward the priest, still crouched to drink, and gave him a hard kick in the shoulder, knocking him to the ground. "I said you've had enough!"

"I'd say *you* have had enough!" The voice seemed to come from out of the sky, and the guards looked at each other with perplexed expressions. Father Olivera likewise looked up to see from where this new voice had come. Then they all saw. A figure whose face was covered below the eyes stood upon the roof of the shrine, where he had been lying in wait. He held a bow out before him, string drawn, and loaded arrow ready to fly.

The bigger guard shouted up, "I don't know what it is you want, but you've picked the wrong men to try and rob today. You're not going to drop both of us with one arrow." Tomi recognized the man as the one who had struck him and forced him to step upon the bronze figure back in Kōnose. And he was the one who branded the farmer's poor daughter with the *fumie*.

The masked figure on the roof hollered back down, "You're right, I can't drop you both." With that, he took quick aim and released the arrow. There was a momentary high-pitched sound of displaced air, and then a loud reverberating thwack. The big man looked down at the foreign object protruding from his sandaled left foot before letting out a long howl. The arrow had pierced through bone and muscle and lodged itself deep into the solid wooden platform beneath.

The smaller guard, sword drawn, rushed forward toward the shrine to get up on the roof before Tomi could nock another arrow. He managed only a few steps before Shirō,

TO SAVE A PRIEST

stepping out from behind the shrine, put a blade up to his throat.

The guard, startled by the sudden appearance of yet a second ambusher, reflexively dropped his own weapon. Shirō scooped up the fallen sword with the top of his sandaled foot, and propelled it toward Father Olivera. The priest was confused, but picked up the blade with his bound hands.

Tomi jumped down from the roof and went over to the guard with the arrow through his foot. The man's teeth were clenched in pain, but any attempt to move seemed to only increase his agony. "I could try to yank it out," said Tomi, "but that might do more damage." He was surprised to see that there was no external bleeding, but the foot was purplish and swollen.

"No," said Shirō, "don't pull it out."

"Well, I wasn't actually planning to," replied Tomi. "I think he's quite secure just as he is."

"Yes, keep an eye on them both," said Shirō. "I'll be back shortly."

Tomi, raising an eyebrow, asked, "Where are you going?"

Shirō didn't answer as he headed toward the woods beyond the boundary of the shrine. He scanned the forest floor, and eventually found what he was looking for—the low-growing, long-leafed wild *ukon* plant that grew in abundance throughout the region. Taking hold of one by the base of its stem, he pulled up gently, removing the entire plant with its roots. He did the same with several more and brought them back to the shrine.

"What are you doing?" asked Tomi.

"I'm making a poultice." Shirō removed the leaves and set them aside. He then laid the roots upon a flat stone and, with the edge of his sword, pressed down against them until they were flat and oozing with a viscous substance. "Hand me the ladle."

Tomi did as he was asked. Shirō placed the crushed root into the ladle, and added just a small amount of water from the fountain. He swirled the mixture around until it achieved a smooth consistency, and then set it aside. He walked over to the big man who, seeing Shirō approach with sword in hand, cried, "What are you doing?"

Shirō replied evenly, "I'm going to cut it. Just be still."

The big man gave a look of fear, as though he thought that, by "it," Shirō might have meant his foot. Taking a firm hold of the arrow with his right hand, Shirō proceeded to gingerly run the length of his sword's blade along the shaft. In just two quick strokes, the arrow was cut. Without any prompting, the big man grimaced as he lifted his foot, freeing it from the portion of the arrow that remained embedded in the wood.

"I was about to ask if we should let them live," said Tomi, "but I'm now guessing I know the answer."

"There is no need for killing," said Shirō as he walked over to Father Olivera and cut his hands loose of their bonds. Seeing the longer length of rope still dangling from the saddle horn of one of the horses, Shirō said, "I have another idea." They forced the two guards to sit with their backs to either side of the hitching post. Then Tomi walked the horse in a circle, as the rope securely bound the two men to the post and to one another. If one of the men struggled to loosen the bond, it only caused the other to moan in greater discomfort. "Someone will be along eventually," Shirō assured them.

Taking up the ladle, he once again approached the big man. "This will lessen the pain and quicken the healing." He then applied the paste to both the top and bottom of the wounded foot. The big man winced and made a sound by sucking in air through his teeth. Handing the big man a bundle of the *ukon* leaves, Shirō said, "Keep these pressed against the wound. It will also help." Then, as if everything he had done had not been curious enough, Shirō laid a hand upon the wounded foot and spoke,

> *"Saint Raphael, the archangel, arrow and medicine of divine love, wound our hearts with the burning love of God, and let this wound never heal, so that we might always remain upon the path of love and overcome all things through love. Amen."*

The big man looked perplexed. "Did you just pray that my wound never heal?"

Shirō smiled behind his mask. "I pray that your wounded foot heals, but that your hardened heart might be transformed by the wound of conversion."

"What sort of strange talk is this?"

The smaller man, all the while, had been loudly issuing a string of curses and threats.

"Shall we take the horses?" asked Tomi. "I think your priest friend has done enough walking for one day."

"No," answered Shirō. "But let's take some sandals for his feet."

Tomi walked over to the bound guards. "Well, it looks like the big one is closer to the right size, but one of his sandals is damaged." Then, looking at the smaller guard, "I guess yours will have to do."

"And," added Shirō, "let's take whatever supplies they have." They opened the saddlebags on the horses, and took the items of food, water flasks, and some torches.

Seeing the torches, Father Olivera said quietly, "They used those to burn the church." It was with those words that Shirō knew that the priest recognized him, despite the face covering.

Shirō turned with wide eyes to face him. "Was anyone

inside, Father?"

"Only the body of a man who was already dead. It was one of the soldiers."

"My heart is heavy to hear this, Shinpu," Shirō said with his eyes to the ground. "We may have need of these torches though." With that, the three gathered their weapons and supplies, and headed quickly back toward the river.

七

INTO THE CAVE
洞窟へ

*"Anyone who has common sense will remember
that the bewilderments of the eyes are of two kinds,
and arise from two causes, either from coming out
of the light or from going into the light."*
Plato, Allegory of the Cave

*"If you do not enter the tiger's cave,
you will not catch its cub."*
Japanese proverb

Father Olivera was weak from the march and from hunger. Though he was accustomed to fasting, his body was not normally subjected to such physical exertion during those times. Tomi ran upstream along the narrow beach to the rock shelf under which the boys had hidden the boat from plain view. He dragged the boat to the edge of the water, and waited for the others to arrive. They secured the weapons and newly acquired supplies, and pushed off back into the water.

When the sight of the *torī* gate became a tiny red speck on the distant shore, Shirō turned to Father Olivera. "Shinpu, are you alright?"

"Yes, I am fine. Just a bit tired." He paused a moment to look at each of the boys, who had removed their face coverings once they reached the boat. "Shirō, you should not have done this. You've put yourself at great risk."

"I think I was already at great risk, Father. In any case, we were not going to let them take you." Shirō realized he had not introduced his friend. "Father, this is Tomi."

"Yes, I remember you, young Ishibara-san, though I've not seen you in quite some time."

"I've been away," replied Tomi.

"Yes, so I had heard."

Tomi turned back to Shirō. "Well, what now? After all that, are we heading all the way to Yatsushiro after all?"

"No."

"Well, what then? Do we get off at Sakamoto?"

"I considered that," answered Shirō, "but I think we should get away from the river. I want to try to get back to Hitoyoshi. I believe Shinpu would be safe at the castle."

"I'm not sure he'll be safe anywhere on our islands, but whatever you think best, Shirō."

"Let's get to the other side of the river. Tomi, do you remember where the mouth of the cave is?"

"The cave? We haven't been there since we were kids. But, yes, I think I remember. Do you?"

"*Hai.*"

The current was strong, and the boat moved ahead quickly. With Shirō at the tiller, and Tomi working with an oar on the port side, they were able to navigate toward the river's opposite shore. They reached a point where the river took a sharp bend to the left. "Here!" Shirō shouted above the noise of the rapids. "Let's put it in here!"

They managed to get the boat onto a stony beach with a

steep slope behind it. Beyond that were bamboo groves that skirted the base of a row of hills that stretched up and into the clouds. "And what about the boat?" asked Tomi.

"We let it go. No point in leaving a sign of where we got out. Let's take everything with us."

They took the weapons and supplies, and shoved the boat back into the rapids. The current swept it greedily away. "Are you alright to walk a bit, Father? It shouldn't be far."

"Yes, I'm alright, Shirō. But where are we going?"

"Follow me."

They climbed the slope and entered into the bamboo grove. The sun was still high in the afternoon sky, but it was beginning its descent. After about half an hour they came to the base of a large hill. "Come, it's this way—to the right."

"Yes," said Tomi. "It has become overgrown, but it should be somewhere around here." Using their weapons, the two youths began to swipe and prod into the vines and weeds that covered the hill's base.

After several minutes of this, Shirō exclaimed, "Here it is!" With a few short strokes of his sword, he cleared a small opening, just enough to crawl into.

"Is it safe?" asked Father Olivera.

"We discovered this cave when we were kids," explained Shirō. "We explored it many times. It is safe, certainly safer than being on the open road right now. There is a passage within that leads nearly all the way to Takazawa village. But first we'll give you a chance to rest."

Shirō led the way by crawling into the opening. "After you, Olivera-san," said Tomi. The three of them inched their way slowly through the dark narrow space.

Father Olivera spoke into the darkness, "How much farther? I don't do too well in confined spaces!"

Shirō's voice came from just a few feet ahead. "Not much

farther, Shinpu. Keep moving!"

After maneuvering themselves through several yards of the narrow and jagged tunnel, they emerged into an open cavern. Father Olivera lay sprawled upon the smooth stone floor, relieved to stretch his limbs and to take fresh air into his lungs. Fresh air. He noticed that this new environment was cool, even refreshing. He opened his eyes, which he'd kept shut inside the passage, and was amazed by what he saw.

The cavern was spacious. At the back of it was a pool, roughly the size of a bath, the water of which shimmered and reflected a cerulean light that came from above. It was a striking hue that reminded the priest of the cobalt tile interior of the Church of São Lourenço in Portugal. It brought to his mind as well the first time he'd gone swimming at night in the Yatsushiro Sea. There was a curious kind of phosphorescence in the water that radiated a bright bluish green when disturbed, and left illuminated trails as his fingers skimmed across the water's surface. What he saw in the cavern, covering the stalactites that adorned its ceiling, looked much like the glow from that nighttime swim.

"This place," Father Olivera spoke more to himself than to the boys, who had already busied themselves taking an inventory of their supplies, "it's quite astonishing."

"Yes," answered Shirō. "We've always thought so. Come and see, there is more." He led the way through a fairly wide passage that led out of the cavern to another space into which sunlight and fresh air entered through a large opening in one of the walls. The base of the opening was a flat shelf which could be easily climbed. Shirō jumped up and motioned for Olivera to follow. The two stood just outside the cavern in a kind of natural courtyard, the boundaries of which were formed by steep walls of rock. A thin stream of water cascaded down one of the walls and formed a rivulet that disappeared into the side of the cave from which they'd just emerged. "You see?" said Shirō. "It's quite beautiful. And the only way to access this place is through the cave."

"How did you discover this?" asked Olivera.

"Quite by chance," answered Tomi, emerging from the cavern behind them. "This cave leads all the way to the outskirts of Takazawa, but Shirō and I were the ones who discovered the way to get this deep inside. We used to come quite often, but I haven't been back here in a long time. How about you, Shirō?"

"No, I haven't been here since you went away, Tomi-kun. It would have seemed strange coming here without you." He walked over to the waterfall, and washed his hands and face in the cool clear water. "Let's stay here a little while and give Shinpu a chance to rest. Then we'll make our way to Takazawa." The three went back into the cavern and sat for a time, eating some of the millet dumplings from the saddlebags.

After washing down a dumpling with a long drink of water, Father Olivera said, "You know, being here rather reminds me of a story about a cave."

"Oh?" replied Tomi. "A story from your country?"

"Actually, it was written long ago by a man from the land of Greece, a land that in some ways at least is much like ours. It's a country of many islands—and fishermen. It produced many great thinkers, as well as warriors."

Tomi asked, "What is the story about?"

"Well, it's about prisoners who are chained and bound inside of a large cave. They have been there all their lives, which they've spent gazing upon shadows cast upon a wall—shadows of objects held up by others in the cave."

"Others?" asked Shirō, who listened as he sat by the edge

of the pool, swirling a finger around in the still water.

"Yes. There are others in the cave who move about freely. They stand behind the prisoners, and hold up various objects of assorted shapes—a book, a vase, a toy horse, and the like. The light from a fire behind them causes shadows of these things to be cast upon the wall before the prisoners. As they do this, they speak the names of the things. With the passage of time, the prisoners come to associate the words they hear with the shadows they perceive."

"That's a rather odd story," said Tomi.

Father Olivera let out a small laugh. "Yes, indeed it is!"

"What is the point of it?" asked Shirō.

"Well, as the story continues, one of the prisoners somehow manages to escape from the cave, and he finds himself for the first time in the world outside. He fumbles about as his eyes, unaccustomed to natural light, cannot see things for what they are. But over time, he gradually comes to recognize reality and the many objects which, hitherto, he had only known by the vague shadows of those things."

"So, that is the end?" asked Shirō. "He escapes from the strange cave and lives out his days in freedom?"

"No, not quite. He remembers his fellow captives in the cave, and feels pity for them. Desiring their liberation, he returns to the cave."

"I hope he at least brought a sword," said Tomi.

Father Olivera laughed again. "Well, it might not have done him much good. You see, his eyes had become accustomed to the world of light, so now he struggled to make his way through the cave, though it had been his home for all those years."

"And then?" asked Tomi.

"He eventually reaches the prisoners and tries to explain to them about the world outside the cave. But they are very suspicious of him because he is fumbling about like a man who is drunk or mad. And because the cave is all they have ever known, they find his claims about the outside world to be quite unbelievable."

"Does he free them from their shackles?" asked Tomi.

"He wishes to do so, but the prisoners are afraid of ending up like him. Rather than risk such a fate, they turn upon him and kill him."

"What?" exclaimed Shirō. "What sort of ending is this? What is the lesson of such a story? When good fortune shines upon you, do not be foolish enough to attempt to share it with others?"

Father Olivera was silent for a short while, then answered, "The story is telling us something about the temporal world in which we dwell. Many of the things held out to us as truths are in reality mere shadows of truth."

"And what might one of these shadows be?" asked Shirō.

Father Olivera considered this for a while. "Take, for example, the widely held conviction that honor can only be restored by taking one's own life."

"Are you referring to *seppuku*?" asked Tomi.

"Yes," replied Olivera. "I have, I'm afraid, been witness to its bloody brutality on more than one occasion."

Shirō interjected, "There are times when a warrior brings dishonor to himself or his liege lord. On such occasions, the lord is within his rights to demand the life of his servant. I daresay any warrior worthy of the name would rather die than live in a state of dishonor."

"A liege lord is within his rights to take that which he himself has bestowed. If he has granted title and sword to one who then brings dishonor to those things, then let them be taken from him. But no earthly lord has the natural right to demand life which he himself has not vouchsafed."

"But are there not crimes for which death is a just punishment?" asked Tomi.

"Crimes, yes," answered Olivera, "but not the mere whim of a liege lord. And while commanding a servant to take his life by his own hand may satisfy some superficial sense of justice, it ultimately cannot offer something of even greater consequence."

"And what is that?" asked Tomi.

Father Olivera answered, "Reconciliation."

Tomi waved his hand as if to shoo away a pesky insect. "Yes, well, I'm going to reconcile these empty flasks with some fresh water," he said, and climbed back outside to the small waterfall.

Just at that moment, Shirō noticed Olivera begin to teeter.

"Shinpu! What is wrong?" Shirō ran forward and caught the man in his arms before he could fall against the hard stone ledge. "My goodness, you're burning up!"

Tomi, hearing the commotion, ran back into the cavern. "What is it?"

"I don't know. He was fine and just suddenly fainted." Shirō could see a sheen of perspiration on the priest's face. "He's got a fever." Reaching down to Olivera's wrist to check his pulse, Shirō noticed a bright red welt on the forearm. "Shinpu, what happened here? Did your captors do this?"

Olivera was weak but conscious. He looked down at his swollen arm. "No. They did not do that, at least not directly. As they dragged me along the path, I was stung by a large hornet. Thankfully it was only one. I'll be fine. I only need to rest a bit."

Tomi offered, "You should have him do *misogi* under the waterfall to break the fever. My father did that to me when I was a kid."

"*Iie*," replied Shirō. "That's actually the worst thing to do. Under that cold water, his body will shiver and raise his body temperature even more."

"Alright," said Tomi. "You're the medical student. I was only trying to help."

"Wasn't there some *shōga* in the saddlebag with the food?" asked Shirō.

Tomi went over and rummaged through the bag. "*Hai,* here's a big root of it." He held up an object with the unmistakable shape that resembled something like a gnarled hand.

"Good," replied Shirō, "It will help."

"While you tend to your friend, I'm going to check and see if the passage to the other end is clear." Tomi was now pulling a torch from one of the other bags.

"I don't know if it's a good idea for you to go alone, Tomi."

"Don't worry, Shirō, I'll be fine. Besides, there won't be much point in making a sick man walk the entire length of the passage, only for us to discover it's blocked."

"Yes, I suppose you're right about that. But do be careful. I don't want to be treating two patients."

Tomi gave Shirō a wink and disappeared into the passage that led away from the cavern.

Shirō broke off a piece of the *shōga*, and set to work making a poultice, much like he had done earlier with the *ukon* leaves. This he applied to the area of the sting. Taking another piece of the root, he shaved off the rough outer skin with the edge of his blade, and handed it to Olivera. A pungent and spicy aroma filled the space.

"Eat this, Shinpu. It will help to counteract the swelling, and bring the fever down." The priest did as he was instructed. Then he reclined upon the stone ledge and fell into a heavy sleep.

At least two hours passed and Tomi had still not returned. Knowing the passage was long and tricky to negotiate in parts, Shirō was not terribly concerned, at least not yet. Still, he offered up a prayer for his old friend's safety.

He went over to Father Olivera and saw that he was awake. "Shinpu, you've slept for a while. How do you feel?"

"Better," replied the priest, propping himself up slightly with his elbows. "I just needed some rest. I think the *shōga* may have helped."

"Yes, I'm sure that it did." Shirō placed the back of his hand against Olivera's forehead. "You're still warm, but the fever is lower. Once Tomi returns, we will get you to Takazawa, where you can get better rest and care."

Olivera asked, "How long has he been gone?"

"All the while you were asleep—a couple of hours, judging from the light. He shouldn't be much longer."

"As long as we're here, would you care to give me your confession?"

"My confession? Here? In this place?"

"Why not? It may be quite some time before we see the inside of a church again!"

"Shinpu, you shouldn't exert yourself unnecessarily. You're still not well."

"I'm well enough to listen." Then he added, "But you needn't feel obliged."

"Well," said Shirō, "considering all that has happened these past few days, perhaps this would be an opportune time." There was a pause of several moments as Shirō collected his thoughts. Then he began, "Bless me, Father, for I have sinned. Yesterday, I took part in the taking of a man's life." Shirō waited for some visible reaction from Father Olivera, but there was none.

"I see. Tell me of the circumstances." Shirō gave a full account of what happened in the church the previous day.

"From your telling, it seems to me your sin is not a mortal one, as you were acting in the defense of life."

"Yes, but it did not begin that way. I was the one who attacked."

"But you were defending the life of another. You were protecting Kumiko."

"I do not believe it was her life he meant to take."

"Perhaps not. But you were protecting her virtue, and that is something as precious as life. For your penance, pray for the soul of that man. Pray daily for him and for all souls who have, through no fault of their own, died without knowing the friendship of Christ."

"*Hai,* Shinpu."

"Is there anything else you need to confess?"

"I disobeyed my father's command to remain at home. He does not know that I am here, nor about anything that has happened."

"It may have been better had you obeyed that command. And, yet, here we are. Be sure to reconcile with your father when you are again in his presence." The priest paused for a moment before continuing. "Is there anything else?"

"I fear some of my thoughts have at times been impure."

"With regards to a girl?"

"Yes. I believe I have loved her for a long time. I often imagine being with her. But sometimes those thoughts drift toward..." The outward expression of such a private thing made Shirō uneasy, but he forced himself to give words to what weighed upon his heart. "The thoughts at times become unchaste."

"When such thoughts arise, ask our Blessed Mother, the Queen of Virtue, for strength. Just as you protected Kumiko's honor with your body, protect it also with your mind."

"*Hai,* Shinpu."

"Is there anything more?"

"I think I may be guilty of the sin of despair."

"Oh? How so?"

"It is difficult to explain. I recognize there is much joy and beauty in this life. I am grateful for the many blessings Our Lord has bestowed upon me. Yet, there is an abiding sadness that seems to hang over me like a dark cloud. I am nearly always aware of its presence. It is like some great void into which I fear all joy and gratitude will be swallowed up and consumed."

"From where do you think this sadness might arise?"

"I do not know. It has been present for nearly as long as I can remember. There are times when it leads me to believe that all endeavors are futile and vain—that this life has no real purpose beyond itself."

"Do you believe this to be so?"

"No. In my mind, I know it is not so. Yet my heart seems often unable to embrace that which my mind has come to accept."

Father Olivera was silent for a few moments before speaking, "*Great are you, O Lord, and greatly to be praised. Great is your power, and of your wisdom there is no end. And man, being a part of your creation, desires to praise you—man, who bears about with him his mortality. Yet man, this part of your creation, desires to praise you. You move us to delight in praising you, for you have made us for yourself, and our hearts are restless until they rest in you.*"

"Is that a prayer?" asked Shirō.

"Of a sort. Those are the words of Saint Augustine. Your heart is restless. Pray earnestly through the intercession of Our Blessed Mother, for no human heart ever knew the depth of sorrow that she endured at the foot of the cross. Your sorrow is an occasion for sin only if it drags you to despair. Rather, pray for the grace that it will allow you to love all the more deeply."

"Yes, Father. I shall try."

"Now, I shall grant you absolution. Is there anything else you need to confess?"

Shirō thought for a moment before answering, "Well, Father, I did steal a boat."

Shortly after Shirō's confession, the light outside began to fade. Father Olivera was sitting up, and Shirō instructed him to drink plenty of water, and to chew on another piece of the *shōga*. The priest half-jokingly responded to the order, saying, "*Hai, sensei!*" using the title reserved for physicians and others who are masters of their disciplines.

From the direction of the passage came a dancing of shadows followed by a human figure. Neither Shirō nor Olivera had heard him approach. It was Tomi. "Have you just returned?" asked Shirō. "I was beginning to become concerned."

"I have been here for a little while now," replied Tomi. "I heard what sounded like some religious ritual, so I stayed back until you two were finished. But the passage is clear. A few spots may require some squeezing or climbing, but it is passable."

"Alright," said Shirō. "The sun is nearly down. I say we stay here tonight, and leave at first light. That will give Shinpu a chance to rest some more, and give us at least a bit less need of the torch oil."

"That's fine by me," said Tomi. Then he added, "Do you two have any more rituals that need performing? Shall I go out to the courtyard to give you some privacy?" There was more than a hint of mockery in his voice.

Shirō answered, "No, Tomi, but thank you for your consideration."

Olivera thought better of it, but he couldn't resist asking, "And how about you, master Ishibara? What would it take to convince you to become a warrior for Iesu?"

Tomi let out a laugh that echoed in the space. "I have little enough use for the religion of my own ancestors. I'm quite sure I have even less for that of yours."

"I see." Olivera thought for a moment. "What if a foreigner offered to teach you an art of combat superior to any of your native land? Would you at least consider such a proposal?"

"Well, first of all, combat is something real—as well as practical. I see nothing useful about the belief in heaven and spirits, and bread that becomes flesh, and all the other things your complicated religion posits. Besides, there is no art of combat any foreigner could teach that is superior to the way taught by master Musashi."

With that, Tomi went out to the courtyard to refill his empty water flask.

"Don't think ill of him, Shinpu," said Shirō. "He means no disrespect."

"No, I'd say he does mean disrespect, but I do not think ill of him," replied Olivera. "Quite the contrary, I believe he has a big heart. He's just searching for something big enough to fill it."

"Yes, I suppose you may be right, on both accounts."

Just then a loud noise came from the passage from which Tomi had earlier emerged. Shirō instinctively reached for his sword.

"What is it?" asked Olivera. But before anyone could answer, the cavern became filled with the fluttering of dozens of bats making their nightly exit from the cave in search of food.

Shirō and Olivera dove to the floor and watched as the dark cloud passed above them and into the courtyard. The next thing they heard was the sound of Tomi shouting as the creatures flew in his direction.

八

UNJUST TAX
不当な税金

*"Why do you make me see iniquity, and cause me
to look on wickedness? Yes, destruction and violence
are before me; strife exists and contention arises."*
Habakkuk 1:3

*"Forgiveness is primarily for our own sake, so that we
no longer carry the burden of resentment. But to forgive
does not mean we will allow injustice again."*
Gautama Buddha

"You must stop shouting!" Kuritani was doing his best
to bring order to a room that was erupting with rage.
Following the events of the previous night, the men of the
village found themselves gathered to decide what action, if
any, they might be able to take. Kuritani, always one of the
most soft-spoken and level-headed men of the village, found
himself in the position of trying to keep inflamed tempers
in check. From the time he was a boy, he was affectionately
called *Shimarisu*, the word for "chipmunk," by most of his
fellow villagers, mainly on account of his plump cheeks.
But no one was calling him by that name on this particular

evening. "Please, Yoshimura-san, we are all in the same situation, and we all understand your feelings."

Yoshimura snapped his head toward Kuritani, who could see the mix of grief and rage that had been pushed to the point of madness. "You understand my feelings? Was it your wife they took?"

The previous day, the regional tax collector, a gaunt-looking fellow named Kasumi, escorted by a band of *samurai* from Yatsushiro Castle, had come to the village to collect the monthly tax of rice. The villagers were all made to report to the common area where fifteen sacks, each filled with five *shō* of uncooked grains of rice, were gathered. Kasumi looked down at the sacks, and then at the faces of the villagers, with a look of disdain. Raising his voice so that all could hear, he bellowed, "Where is the rest? This is scarcely half of what is due!" The villagers were silent, their heads and eyes cast to the ground. Kasumi paced back and forth, his thin lips pursed, looking increasingly agitated as he continued to gaze at the rice sacks. Each was tied shut with a short length of twine. He repeated the question more insistently, "Where is the rest?"

It was then that Yoshimura stepped forward. "Please, sir. The crop is very poor this year. You know that the summer was exceptionally dry. What you see here is all that we have. We scarcely have enough to feed ourselves."

The collector ceased his pacing and silently regarded Yoshimura for a moment. "Is that so?" He then looked upon the *butsudan* shrine that stood at the edge of the common area. The ceramic Buddha within had been removed and replaced with a wooden cross bearing the image of the crucified Iesu. A smirk came over Kasumi's face. "I see you are followers of the *kirisutokyō* cult. Isn't it true that you rest one day of every seven? How many more sacks might there be if not for this gratuitous day of leisure you permit yourselves?"

Yoshimura answered, "Sir, even the Buddha observed the *uposatha*. A body requires rest to be able to work the fields the remainder of the week. We are weak as it is for lack of food."

The collector looked with beady eyes under sparse brows at Yoshimura, and then scanned the crowd. He returned his gaze to Yoshimura, and then to Yoshimura's young wife who had been standing quietly behind him. She was six months along with their first child. "I see the malnutrition you claim is not so bad as to prevent you from breeding." He took hold of Yoshimura's wife by the wrist and pulled her to himself.

Yoshimura rushed forward to her defense, but the *samurai* reacted immediately, their swords drawn and levelled at Yoshimura and the other men who had moved in protest. Kasumi grinned and addressed Yoshimura, loudly enough so that all could hear. "Since you are so short on rice for yourselves, I will alleviate some of your burden by taking this woman into my care. Do not worry, I shall make certain she is properly nourished."

Yoshimura lunged toward the collector. One of the *samurai* thrust the hilt of his sword into Yoshimura's stomach, sending him to the ground in a heap. Kasumi, with his captive firmly in his grasp, addressed the crowd. "Once you lazy peasants have gathered the remainder of what you owe, you are to deliver it to the castle. Until that time, this woman shall remain with me."

He walked with wide strides to the *butsudan* and laid hold of the cross inside. Raising it up, he shouted, "If any of these, or any other of your *kirisutokyō* images are seen again, everyone in this village will pay—with something far more dear than rice!"

With that, he motioned to one of the *samurai*, and then

threw the cross high into the air. The soldier drew his sword and, with one clean decisive stroke, deftly cleaved the piece of wood in two. The halves fell to the earth, and the soldiers mounted their horses.

The villagers ran about in a state of hysteria. Yoshimura's wife, who had fallen silent, was forced to sit in front of Kasumi upon his own horse. As the band of marauders rode off, Yoshimura picked himself up from the dirt and began in vain to chase after them. He ran through the cloud of dust left upon the path until his legs and lungs burned and he could go no further. Sinking again to his knees, he wept bitterly.

At dawn, several of the women gathered around the *butsudan* to pray. One of them had attempted to repair the severed crucifix with a smearing of sticky rice from the remnants of her previous morning's meager breakfast, before resting it gently back into the wooden structure. The women who had them took out small ropes fashioned into a circle and adorned with small beads made from knotted bamboo leaves. They proceeded to pray for the welfare of their abducted kinswoman and her unborn child. They prayed also for the strength to bear their crosses. They prayed even for their persecutors.

Meanwhile, the men gathered in the home of Kuritani to discuss what action might be taken. It didn't take long to become plain that there were two opposed camps. Roughly half of the men, enraged by the barbarous act of the abduction, wished to take up arms and attempt to rescue Yoshimura's wife by force. Many of them, though they had been farmers for several years, had once been *samurai*. In some cases, their conversion had caused them to be dismissed by their lords, who found the foreign religion distasteful and at odds with the warrior code of *bushido*. Others had simply been dismissed for economic reasons: their feudal lord was unable or unwilling to feed them. In either case, the loss of official position made them *rōnin*—literally, "wanderers," warriors without a master. But a *samurai* was a *samurai* for life, and Iesu had become their new master. And they pledged by their new creed to serve him as faithfully as they could. And though they accepted their new occupations with glad hearts, still they made every possible opportunity to train amongst themselves to keep their skills honed.

One such of these, Hashizume, assumed the role of spokesman for this group. Hashizume was well known in the region. He had distinguished himself in several battles of the Sengoku War, as well as the invasion of Kankoku. But he was perhaps best known by his appearance, one that made him easy to identify even from a distance. He was considerably darker than most of his countrymen, and his face had a look of worn leather. Once after *Misa* in Hitoyoshi, Father Olivera had shown some Spanish artwork that depicted native people of Mexico. Someone had remarked, "Hashizume, you look like you'd fit right in with their tribe!" Hashizume was not amused.

Now Hashizume, the one who resembled a warrior from a faraway land, spoke: "That we are patiently enduring the yoke of these excessive taxes is one thing. But yesterday's offense cries to heaven for justice. As many of you too well know, this was not an isolated incident. My own niece in Kōnose, the eldest daughter of my brother, was branded with a *fumie* when my brother refused to tread upon it. The abuses are becoming more common, and they will only get worse. Now is the time to stand in defense of our honor, and that of our women and children!"

Kuritani turned to face him. "What do you mean, stand in defense? Just what are you saying?"

"I'm saying that our hand has finally been forced. When the collector took Yoshimura's wife, he didn't take her as collateral for the tax, though that would have been villainous enough. He knows full well that there is no more grain to harvest. No, he took her out of pure malice, to satisfy his own lusts and to wound our spirits. If we cower like beaten dogs, a precedent will be set, and our situation will only worsen. Any time their capricious conditions aren't met, they will feel at liberty to torture and abuse. And then there is the further matter of the prohibition of the faith at the whim of the *shōgun*. Are we to deny the faith to our children because we are too afraid to take a stand?"

"You can't pass along the faith to anyone if you're dead," replied Kuritani.

Several of the men grunted in agreement.

"Death will come to us all, one way or another," answered Hashizume. "But even a rabbit will bite when he is cornered," he added, quoting the old Chinese proverb.

Kuritani shook his head in exasperation. "What precisely is it you would have us do?"

"I do not know exactly. But I do know that if all the men of the Christian villages rally together, we would be a force of over *ichi-man*."*

A murmur began to swell in the room, but Kuritani quickly interrupted. "And do you think for a moment that Tokugawa doesn't have ten times that number at his disposal? And his soldiers are well supplied and trained ... and well fed."

"Yes, but those soldiers wouldn't be fighting with the same resolve that we possess."

"You do realize that any form of protest, armed or otherwise, would be seen as insurrection. It would be

*Ten thousand.

tantamount to suicide."

"As I said, every man eventually meets his end. I would prefer a swift death with honor over death by a thousand cuts. And there is something else to consider. It is possible that, when the Iberians see the gravity of our plight, they may come to the aid of their fellow believers."

"That may be very wishful thinking," answered Kuritani. "After all, the priests are being expelled, and there seems to be no response from the bishop of Macau or anyone else."

"Aid may yet be forthcoming," offered Hashizume. "In the meantime, we need to organize."

There was a prolonged silence as the men pondered all that had been spoken. Then everyone in the room stiffened and cocked their heads as they heard the sound of the women shouting outside.

九

CHOSEN
選ばれた

*"Speak up for those who cannot speak for themselves,
for the rights of all who are destitute. Speak up and judge
fairly; defend the rights of the poor and needy."*
Proverbs 31:8-9

*"Only he who knows his own weaknesses
can endure those of others."*
Japanese proverb

As the three companions emerged from the cave, they were blinded by the light of the rising sun directly before them. Squinting and raising their hands to shield their eyes, they took small steps to avoid stumbling over anything upon the ground which they could not yet clearly perceive. Father Olivera drew in a deep breath of the crisp air and felt a surge of vitality return to his limbs. His fever had broken, and the swelling from the hornet's sting was now nearly indiscernible.

As they made their way along the path in the direction of the village, they spied a group of human figures seated upon the ground. A sound like chanting could be heard. As

93

they drew nearer, Father Olivera and Shirō recognized that they were hearing the recitation of the *Rozario*. Most of the women of the village were gathered there. One of the women spotted the three men as they approached. She pointed at them and began to shout.

When the men of the village arrived on the scene, they saw that the women were in a frenzy as they surrounded a man who was not of the village yet familiar to them. Though they did not immediately recognize him without his vestments, the men soon realized that it was Father Manuel Olivera.

"Shinpu!" one of them exclaimed, "We feared the worst had befallen you!" Olivera tried to respond, but he could not make himself heard above the noise of the women. They were embracing his legs and sobbing like mothers whose sons, believed to be slain in battle, had returned beyond hope safely home.

Shirō and Tomi stood at a short distance, content to be observers of this impassioned reception. One of the men, looking upon Shirō, said, "Young master Nakagawa? Is that you?"

Shirō replied, "*Hai, Nakagawa desu.*"*

The women were still carrying on, and it became clear that several of them were asking for Olivera to hear their confessions. One of the men broke through the circle and firmly placed a protective arm over the priest's shoulder. Chiding the women, he said, "Let the man rest! Can't you see he's been through an ordeal?"

With that, Father Olivera and his two young companions were escorted to Kuratani's home, from which the men had just abruptly departed, and offered tea and a small portion of pottage.

---

*"Yes, it is Nakagawa."

"I am sorry we have so little to offer," said Kuratani. "All of the rice was taken yesterday."

"*Iie, iie,*" replied Father Olivera, and held up a hand to deflect the apology. "It is we who must apologize for our intrusion. We are most grateful for your hospitality." After they had eaten, stories were exchanged concerning the events of the past few days.

"We saw smoke rising out of Hitoyoshi from across the valley," said Kuritani. "We were uncertain of the source of the fire, but after hearing accounts of what has been happening in the region, we suspected it was the church. And we feared the worst as to your fate."

"I am grateful to be among the living, among friends. However, my presence here puts you all at great risk. It will be better for you that I move on."

Hashizume spoke. "*Iie.* We will not send you away. You shall remain here under our protection."

"Protection?" one of the others interrupted. "How can we protect Shinpu when we can't even protect our own?"

Hashizume ignored the question and continued, "The people are starved for absolution and for the body of our Lord. Please remain with us, Shinpu. We will keep your presence hidden as best we are able."

Father Olivera gave a half laugh. "You know it will be nearly impossible to hide a *gaijin*! No, I cannot put your lives in danger. I am a fugitive now."

"A fugitive. Yes, perhaps. But for us, you are a physician. And we are in need of healing. You will remain here, Shinpu. At least for now."

Realizing there was no use in arguing the point, Olivera let it go for the time being. There was much discussion about all that was happening in the region—the unjust taxation, the abuses, and the abduction of Yoshimura's wife.

"What will you do?" asked Shirō, addressing the men.

"We will pray for the grace to carry our cross with patience," answered Kuritani. "And we shall pray for our enemies."

"I can pray for my enemies even while I smite them," said Hashizume.

Tomi spoke up. "So what are you planning? Leading an army of farmers against the lord of Yatsushiro?"

"There are many of us able to fight," answered Hashizume. "We wielded the sword long before the hoe and reaping knife."

Shirō, who had been quietly listening, asked, "Might it be possible to reason with the lord of Yatsushiro Castle?"

The room fell silent and all eyes were on Shirō. "Reason?" asked Kuritani.

"Clearly the taking of Yoshimura-san's wife was unlawful. That she is with child makes the crime all the more disgraceful. For failure to pay the levied tax, a *daimyō* would be within his rights to withhold protection from the village. But the abduction of a citizen for what amounts to a ransom is not his legal right."

"Would you go to Yatsushiro on our behalf, Master Shirō?" asked Kuritani.

Shirō was taken off guard by the question. "On your behalf?"

"Your family is known and respected," answered Kuritani. "You are an educated and learned young man. None of us are of any station. Even the *rōnin* amongst us have no more status than the rest. But you are *samurai*. You could petition Lord Matsui on our behalf."

Shirō answered, "I am in no position to speak on anyone's behalf. And even if I were, there may well be a price on my head for assaulting soldiers from the castle."

Tomi leaned in toward Shirō and said, "They didn't see our faces."

"Yes, I suppose that is true," said Shirō, "Still, there is little reason to believe Lord Matsui would be moved by any petition I might present."

Kuritani turned toward Shirō and offered a gentle bow. "*Sumimasen*, Master Shirō. I know what I propose is much to ask. Perhaps it is presumptuous of me to make such a request. But your intercession just might convince Lord Matsui to order the release of our kinswoman. I humbly implore only that you pray upon the matter."

Shirō was moved. "Yes, brother, I will do this." Then he asked, "What is the name of Yoshimura-san's wife?"

"Her given name is Mariko. But on her baptism, she took the name of Maria."

It was late into the night, and Shirō and Tomi began to feel the events of the past two days catch up to them. They lay upon the straw mats that were offered them, and sleep quickly overtook them. Shirō's sleep was especially deep, and he dreamed.

In the dream, he saw himself once again on the river. He was standing in the boat, looking out upon the flowing waters, and admiring the beauty of the clouds spread out across a seemingly endless sky. He turned to speak to Tomi, but realized there was no one else with him. He looked down and discovered that there was in fact no boat. He was simply standing upon the water and gliding, as some invisible force kept him afloat and moving forward.

Still looking down, a feeling of fear began to come upon him. The rational part of him knew he should not be standing on water, and he was afraid that he might plunge beneath the surface at any moment. But then his attention was drawn back toward the sky. He noticed that one of the clouds directly above him began to take the shape of a large bird. The cloud appeared to be descending and moving directly toward him.

As it drew nearer, it became more distinct in form, until finally he could see that it was not a cloud but rather a dove. As it flew nearer to him and came within reach, Shirō lifted up his arm. This was initially a move to defend himself from the creature, lest it should attack. But he saw there was nothing aggressive in its manner, so he opened his hand and allowed the bird to rest in his palm. Shirō and the bird regarded one another. The dove tilted its head slightly to one side and, for a moment, Shirō thought perhaps the creature might speak. But it did not. Instead, it simply flew away, leaving Shirō with a feeling of sadness.

He stretched out his arm in the hopes it might come back to him. It did not. But when he looked in his hand, he saw that there was an egg. He stared at it with fascination and, upon its shell, he could see the image of a woman's face. She had an expression of deep love, but at the same time one of great sorrow. Her eyes were welled with tears. Shirō closed his hand gently around the egg lest it should fall into the water. He held it close to his chest as he continued to float along the river.

十

Voice of Reason
理性の声

"And whosoever shall not receive you, nor hear your words, going forth out of that house or city, shake off the dust from your feet."
Matthew 10:14

"The go-between wears out a thousand sandals."
Japanese proverb

"I believe the dream was a sign that I should go," Shirō said to Tomi as the two of them sat down to the small breakfast of fish broth, yams, fermented soybeans, and a few slices of *daikon* radishes, prepared for them by some of the women. "I was on the river heading in the direction of Yatsushiro."

Tomi looked unconvinced. "Dreams are the mind's way of patching together a story from all the loose thoughts floating around inside it. You dreamed of the river because we were just on it."

"And the dove and the egg?"

"You were hungry."

Shirō laughed. "Yes, perhaps. But I've decided to go."

"I think that unwise, Shirō. You have little reason to expect favorable treatment. You may wear the swords, but you also wear that cross, and you see what is happening."

"Yes, I do see. But I believe Lord Matsui might at least give my request a *tatemae* level of consideration," *Tatemae* was the word used to describe one's outward expression of a given reaction. Its counterpart, *hon'ne*, was the term for one's true feelings, not always sufficiently dignified for public display.

"I wouldn't be so certain," retorted Tomi. "You know me, I say what's on my mind. Frankly, I think you're foolish to involve yourself in the affairs of these people. Their taxes, and the penalty for not paying them, are their own concern."

"Tomi, this isn't just about taxes. One of their women was taken. That's someone's daughter, someone's wife. They asked me to speak on their behalf. How can I refuse?"

"Quite easily. Just go back home. I'd say you've done enough good deeds for one week."

Shirō looked down at the empty bowl before him. "Tomi, there is more happening here than the mistreatment of one village. You know this to be true. You've witnessed it for yourself. The plight of the peasants is connected to the persecution of the religion I profess. Up to now, the practice of my faith has been little more than an intellectual exercise. When I saw Kumiko slip into the church under the cover of night to consume those consecrated hosts, I realized she had a depth of faith that I did not. She was willing to sacrifice her body, her very life, for the sake of something greater. I have never been asked to sacrifice anything for the cause of the faith—until now."

Tomi threw up his hands. "I don't get it, Shirō. What is this allegiance you hold to this religion? As far as I'm concerned, religion is little more than being told what to think by someone else. You shouldn't allow your thoughts to be dictated by anyone else!"

Shirō looked directly at his friend. "If I'm not mistaken, Tomi, it seems you're trying to dictate to me how I should think."

Tomi appeared taken aback by this response. He was about to say something, but Shirō spoke first.

"When we were kids, you stepped in when a bully was about to pummel me. What I want to do for these people is really no different."

"Yes, well, I had nothing to lose. But you do. You're *samurai*. Your family has status. You're on the path to becoming a doctor. Don't risk losing all that for things that are beyond your control."

"Like I said, Tomi, it's precisely because I have something to lose that I must risk it."

"Alright, Shirō. I see you've made your decision. I think you're a fool, but if you're so set on going, I'm going with you."

"No, Tomi. I think it better if you didn't. We're more likely to be recognized if we are together. I have to believe our two friends from the river managed to make it back to the castle one way or another."

Tomi protested, but finally agreed that Shirō might be correct on this point.

The villagers gave Shirō a flask of water and some boiled yams for the half-day's walk to Yatsushiro. He would travel along the path that followed the river.

Father Olivera was also up and about. "Do take care, Shirō. Are you quite certain you wish to do this?"

"*Hai*, Shinpu. I believe I may be able to help these people. I must at least try to return Maria-san to the village."

Olivera held up a silver chain from which hung a small pendant. "I was surprised the soldiers didn't tear this from my neck, but I'd like for you to carry it. It's a medal of Christopher, patron saint of travelers. I pray for his intercession to watch over you on your journey. May you return to us swiftly and safely."

Shirō took the pendant and bowed. "*Arigatō*, Shinpu. But I am more concerned for your welfare. You must take pains to stay out of sight."

"*Hai*, Shirō-san, I shall."

Shirō walked north, the same direction as the river's current, on the road that ran alongside the Kuma. He normally enjoyed time spent alone, but his mind was cluttered with so many thoughts that were swirling about and colliding into one another. He quickened his pace, thinking perhaps he could somehow get ahead of his own mind. But the acceleration of his limbs only hastened the thoughts. He decided to employ an opposite approach, and came to a complete halt.

The sunlight glistened as it danced across the rippled surface of the river. Shirō walked down to the water's edge and sat upon a smooth stone. He closed his eyes and listened for a while to the sound of the current. There was a blend of low and high pitches that reverberated against the river's rocky banks. Shirō found this sound to be quite soothing. It had a particular cadence, and soon the rate of his own breathing settled into the same rhythm.

He began to pray, "Lord, I do not grasp why you permit the persecution of your people, though I know that the world hated you first. If I cannot possess the wisdom of complete understanding, please grant at least the trust in the goodness of your ways, and the courage to follow them. Shirō opened his eyes and looked down at the medal dangling at his chest. Clasping the small pendant in his hand, he said, "Saint Christopher, pray for me, and for all travelers in this life."

As he was about to stand, Shirō spied the bright blue plumage of a *kawasemi* perched upon a branch hanging over the water. It dove straight down, its long pointed beak piercing the river's surface like an arrow. In an instant, it came back up with a small fish and returned to the branch. It swallowed its catch, and then momentarily regarded Shirō before flying out of sight.

It was still well before dusk when Shirō arrived at the Yatsushiro castle grounds. The original castle's main keep and *yagura* turrets had been leveled in an earthquake two years before Shirō was born. But the outer walls remained, for the most part, intact. Throughout the country, each feudal domain, or *han* as they were called, was home to one castle for its sovereign lord. But in the region of Kumamoto, it was determined that a second fort would be necessary to ensure the protection and security of the port areas. So it was that Iemitsu Tokugawa had sent Lord Matsui to Yatsushiro to rebuild and occupy the castle there. And Matsui was given license to tax the people as heavily as necessary to ensure the timely completion of the task. He was encouraged to lean particularly hard on the Christian villages, imposing upon them even birth and death taxes.

It had been some time since Shirō had visited Yatsushiro. He had nearly forgotten just how long and expansive the stone walls of the massive fortress were. They enclosed a space nearly equal in area to that of Shirō's entire village. As he approached, he could see the rising framework of the newly constructed main keep and several other auxiliary structures. The rectangular fortress was abutted on two sides by water. The Kuma River ran parallel to the long southern wall just before emptying into the bay, which bordered the shorter western wall. A sturdy wooden bridge built upon stone piers allowed access over the river to the main gate of the fortress. Shirō stepped onto the bridge and made his solitary crossing.

He was met at the gate by three guards. Shirō thought there was something familiar about the one who addressed him. "What is your business?"

"I seek an audience with Lord Matsui."

"On whose behalf and on what matter?"

"I come on behalf of the village of Takazawa."

"On whose orders? Do you have papers?"

"I do not. I realize I come unannounced, but I do beg an audience with Lord Matsui. I am the son of Hiromu Nakagawa. My father and Lord Matsui fought together in the Imjin Wars."

The guards eyed Shirō with wariness. The one who seemed familiar to Shirō ordered him to wait. He entered the gate and returned after a short while. "Lord Matsui will see you." Shirō offered a deep bow to the guard, who in turn gave a cursory tilt of the head.

"Leave your swords," said one of the other guards. Shirō surrendered them and was escorted into the castle by the guard who, for a reason Shirō could still not quite ascertain, seemed familiar. As they walked through a wide corridor, a group of soldiers came walking toward them. They looked at Shirō but paid him little mind.

But one of them stopped just as he made eye contact. "I know you," said the man. And Shirō immediately saw that it was Lord Onizuka. "You were at the church in Hitoyoshi."

"*Hai*," replied Shirō.

"Why are you here, Christian?"

"I have come to offer my services to Lord Matsui."

Onizuka laughed. "Your services? I'm certain he has enough girls to serve his tea!"

"Then I shall have to be of service in some other way," answered Shirō.

Onizuka looked Shirō up and down and laughed. "I don't know what that way might be. I don't believe Lord Matsui likes young boys, but perhaps he'd make an exception for one as pretty as you." The other soldiers joined in the laughter.

"*Sumimasen*," said Shirō, "Have I given some cause for your insults?"

The smile disappeared from Onizuka's face. "The cross you wear is cause enough for insult." He reached up to grab a hold of it.

But before he could, the guard escorting Shirō interrupted. "Come! Lord Matsui awaits."

Shirō bowed to Onizuka and stepped slowly backwards before turning away. Onizuka called to him, "Your priest has gone missing. You were there when he was arrested, but somehow he managed to escape. He was aided by two men who attacked my soldiers. Do you know where the priest is now?"

Shirō turned to face Onizuka. "I do not." Indeed, Shirō did not know precisely where Father Olivera was at that moment, though he assumed it was probably somewhere within the village.

"Be assured, he will be found."

Shirō did not reply, but simply bowed again and walked away.

At the end of the corridor was a sliding wooden door at which stood two more guards. The one escorting Shirō nodded to them, and they slid the doors open. Shirō walked through and into a spacious room with a high vaulted ceiling.

There were but a few items situated sparsely throughout. A low table upon which rested a vase with an arrangement of dried flowers was off to one side. On the opposite side a *shamisen* lay upon the floor with an ivory plectrum beside it. At the far end of the room was a dais upon which Lord Matsui sat behind a low, beautifully crafted, lacquered table.

Shirō stood and gave a deep bow. "Peace upon this home and those who dwell within."

Tsuyoshi Matsui was a handsome and intense looking man. He was tall and slender with a perfectly sculpted chin and cheekbones. A full head of shoulder-length hair fell neatly around either side of his wide forehead. Though the same age as Shirō's father, he had the look of a man ten years his junior. When he spoke, his prominent neck triangle bobbed in unison with the slight flaring of his nostrils. His eyes projected a severity behind which, if one gazed deeply enough, seemed to lie a hidden mischievousness. He invited Shirō to sit and to enjoy some hot tea and crispy *senbei* rice crackers.

"So, you are Hiromu's boy?"

"*Hai*, Matsui-sama. And I thank you for admitting me."

"How is your family? I understand your father is still in the service of Lord Yanazume."

"They are well, my lord. They await the arrival of another child in the spring."

"Well, that is good news! You shall be *onīsan*. With the difference in age, you shall have much to teach your new sibling. So, what are your aspirations, young man?"

"I spent last year studying medicine in Amakusa. I hope to continue along that path."

"Ah, a warrior physician perhaps?" Matsui's smile revealed deep dimples. "Will you engage in the fighting arts one day, and the healing arts the next?"

"I should hope to do whatever my duty requires," replied Shirō.

"A sound answer." Matsui took a sip of his tea. "And have you considered offering yourself as a retainer? Have you perhaps come to Yatsushiro to offer your services here?"

"I had actually considered the seminary."

"You wish to become a *bonze*?"

"Actually, I was referring to the seminary on Amakusa."

Matsui's face sank. "You mean *kirisutokyō*?"

"*Hai.*"

"I'm sorry to be the bearer of bad news, but your timing is rather ill-advised." Matsui placed his cup upon the table and scratched lightly at the side of his neck. "Have you not heard that the new *shōgun* is expelling the foreign priests and instituting a ban on the practice of *kirisutokyō*? This will include even the *daimyō* who made the poor choice to convert."

"I have only recently learned of this, though I hope he might reconsider."

Matsui laughed. "There are few things the elder Tokugawa ever reconsidered. And that is even truer of his son." His smile again evaporated as quickly as it had appeared. "Twenty six crucified Christians should be sufficient evidence of his resolve."

"Yes," said Shirō. "Of this have I also only recently learned."

"The leader among them was one who took the Christian name, Paul Miki. I knew his father. He had been a military advisor to the *shōgun*. The family is quite wealthy and Paul could have taken on any number of occupations. But he chose to enter the Jesuit seminary."

"And is this the crime for which his life was demanded?" asked Shirō.

Matsui squinted his eyes. "A Spanish ship ran aground off the coast near Nagoya. When the authorities boarded, they discovered it was carrying a good deal of artillery. They naturally questioned the Spanish captain about this. His reply was quite astonishing. He boasted that the missionaries were simply paving the way for an eventual conquest by the Spanish and Portuguese. When word of this reached Tokugawa, well, you can imagine his reaction."

"Do you believe the Spanish captain's claim to be true?" asked Shirō. "It seems to me that, were military conquest the intention of the Iberians, they could have achieved this long ago."

"I only know what was reported to me. I also understand the captain was a drunkard, so who knows if what he spoke was true. At any rate, it involves matters beyond my control. It is, therefore, of little concern to me."

"And the execution of young children? Is that also of little concern to you, Matsui-sama?"

There was a flash of anger in Matsui's eyes as he opened his mouth to reply. But he stopped himself. He looked down at his teacup as his dimpled smile returned to his face.

"You strike me as a bright young man. Let me ask you, what is it about this foreign religion that so appeals to you? I can understand, perhaps, why it gives many of the peasants hope—meaning to their perceived sufferings, a promise of eternal paradise in the hereafter, and so on. I can even understand why many of the *daimyō* chose to become practitioners—in order to curry favor with the Spanish and Portuguese traders. Personally, I think allowing the missionaries to build churches and evangelize was an unnecessary concession, though I suspect it may have been done partly to diffuse the political influence of the *bonzes*. But why you, young Nakagawa?"

Shirō was silent for several moments before answering, "I

have come to believe in The Way because it leads to the one who is truth."

"Truth?" Matsui tilted his head back slightly and let out a laugh. "Are you suggesting we did not have truth before the missionaries arrived? When a man's words reflect reality, is that not truth?"

"Yes, but there is also a greater truth."

Matsui looked as though he was about to ask what this 'greater truth' might be, but instead said, "I have studied a bit about this religion you've adopted. I've always considered it wise to know the ways of others, even one's enemies. Especially one's enemies."

"Do you regard Christians as your enemies?" asked Shirō.

"Up until now, no. But if the *shōgun* declares Christianity to be an enemy of the empire, then I must also regard it as so." Matsui filled Shirō's cup as well as his own. The guards who had been standing at the door continued to stare blankly in their general direction. "But I am curious, how do you reconcile this religion with the ancient beliefs of our people? For example, the Christian creation story differs from what we believe about the origin of our own islands. Which do you hold to be true?"

"Our native Shintō teaches that the deity, Izanagi, dipped his jeweled spear into the waters, and the drops that fell from its tip formed the islands of our homeland. The Christian account tells of an all-powerful being, who exists outside and above nature and time, who formed from the abyss the cosmos and all it contains. I believe that the Shintō account is not a contradiction, but rather a reflection of the greater reality."

"I see." Matsui took his cup and gently swirled it in his hand. He watched the leaves as they circled at the bottom. "And what do you believe with regards to the emperor's divinity? Do you deny that he is a direct descendant of the sun goddess, Amaterasu?"

"The source of the emperor's natural authority, and indeed all legitimate earthly authority, comes from the one true God. I wish only that the emperor would have exercised his divine authority, rather than spend his days walled up at the palace in Edo, emerging only for the occasional ceremony, while surrendering his authority to men who rule by ambition rather than for love of their subjects."

"Those are rather bold words coming from one so young as yourself. I admire your candor, though I would advise you to govern the expression of such thoughts. They could easily bring about your premature demise."

"Forgive me, Matsui-sama. I do have a tendency to say more than perhaps I ought."

Matsui again smiled. "No need for apologies. You were simply answering my questions. I only urge you to be cautious. These are particularly dangerous times, especially for anyone wearing one of those." He pointed with his chin to the cross around Shirō's neck. "So, you say the emperor's authority has a divine source, but you do not believe the emperor himself to be a god. You claim that only one man, the one you call Iesu, is truly god, yes?"

"*Hai.* I believe Iesu is the one true God incarnate."

"Why do you believe that your Christian God chose to become a man?"

"There is much to be said in answer to this question. But one reason was so that, by partaking in our humanity, we might share in his divinity."

"If your god desired that the people of our islands share in his divinity, why did he not come here as one of us?"

"But he did come as one of us," replied Shirō. "He came as a man."

Matsui uttered a dissatisfied grunt. "Frankly, I find many of the claims of your religion to be quite incredible."

"*Hai,* they are incredible. They are, indeed, so incredible as to lead one to believe that they must be true. Even given his great powers of imagination, man could not conjure up such things on his own. There are many things that exceed our ability to reason. But that does not in itself make those things unreasonable."

Matsui released an exasperated sigh. "What is in it for you, young man? How can it profit you to cling to this religion? What have you to gain?"

"Happiness," answered Shirō, "in this life and happiness eternal in the next."

"Given the current turning of the tide, I'd say it could bring you little else other than misery. Besides, don't you think that preoccupation with the hereafter can distract a man from enjoying all that this life has to offer?"

Shirō considered this question. "I believe it's quite the contrary. Certainty of one's desired destination is what allows a man to remain on the right path. On my journey here from Takazawa, the eyes of my mind were fixed upon my arrival here at the castle, but that did not lessen my enjoyment of the beauty of the river and the hills taken in by the eyes in my head."

Matsui smiled. "You're an interesting young man, master Nakagawa, though I believe you have a mind that could be better applied to more practical matters. I encourage you to focus on your study of the healing arts, and sever your ties to the foreign religion. I personally bear no malice toward the Christians. But Tokugawa is firm in his resolve, and the will of my master must also be my own will."

"*Hai,*" replied Shirō. "This is something I well understand."

"So what does bring you to Yatsushiro? Are you here on some errand, or just a young man coming to enjoy the pleasures of the city? Surely you did not come just to speak with me about matters of *shingaku*. You say you came from Takazawa. What is your affiliation with that village?"

"I was travelling through the countryside, as I often do. I came to the village seeking some rest and refreshment. But as I arrived, the people were deeply distraught. They shared with me their tale of mistreatment by the tax collector from the castle. They asked if I might be able to plead on their behalf."

"Mistreatment? What sort of mistreatment?"

"In addition to taking what little rice the people had to feed themselves, the collector also took one of the women of the village—a wife and expecting mother."

Matsui stiffened. "Yes, well, my understanding is that the woman asked to go with Kasumi."

"I wonder, why would she do such a thing?"

"She apparently wanted to go where she could be better fed and cared for."

"My lord, do you believe this to be true?"

"Are you suggesting that someone in my service is a liar?"

"Forgive me, Matsui-sama. But I must put forth the question. If it were true that this woman were so desperate that she would abandon her own village, family, and husband, what would that say about the conditions under which the people are living? And if it is not true, as all the people of the village could testify, then it seems that your man has not given a truthful account."

With this, Matsui set his empty cup, upside-down, hard upon the table. "Young man, I have heard enough. As regional tax collector, Kasumi has the authority to deal in a manner he deems necessary with those who fail to make due payment. The woman will be sufficiently cared for and returned once the balance is settled. I depart in two days on a journey to Kyōto. Iemitsu Tokugawa has summoned all the *daimyō* there for the ceremony of his official installation and, sadly, the funeral of his father. The emperor emeritus will of course emerge from his walled up palace in Edo, particularly considering Hidetada was his father-in-law, as well as the empress's grandfather. Several matters, including the fate of your religion and expulsion of the missionaries, will be addressed. You might best serve the people of Takazawa and others by warning them that their little dalliance with *kirisutokyō* has come to an end."

"My lord, please at least allow me to return the woman to the village. I believe you know it was wrong for her to have been taken."

With this, Matsui's eyebrows lowered and drew together. "Do not, young man, presume to tell me what I know. I have enjoyed our time together, but now this discussion is over."

十一

Lost Sons and Daughters
失われた息子と娘

*"If the world hates you, keep in mind that
it hated me first."*
John 15:18

"This dewdrop world is a dewdrop world, and yet..."
Issa Kobayashi

"I'm afraid I do not come bearing good news." The young woman had her eyes to the ground as she spoke to the couple standing before her in one of the castle's common areas.

"Tell us." Michiko feared the worst from Kumiko's tone and slumped posture. She had arrived early in the morning to seek out Shirō's parents at Hitoyoshi Castle. She felt they had a right to know their son's whereabouts and the details of the situation into which he had landed himself. She told them of the events in the church the previous night, and the arrival of an old friend with whom Shirō had set off in search of Father Olivera.

Michiko asked, "Do you know the name of this friend?"

"*Hai*. His name is Ishibara. Tomi Ishibara."

Hiromu and Michiko looked at one another with expressions of disquiet. Tomi had been Shirō's friend from the time he was about seven years old. Tomi was three years older than Shirō and had a recklessness about him. It was not accompanied by any malice, but Michiko had expressed a concern that Tomi might be a bad influence on Shirō or, at the very least, lead him into some situation that would land him in harm's way. Hiromu sometimes shared this concern, but he also believed it would do Shirō good to have an older companion. Tomi was like an older brother to Shirō and, though he was rough around the edges, Tomi always meant well.

Hiromu and Michiko recalled a time when Obāsan was coming into the house from the garden carrying a rather large *suika* that had been ripening in the sun for several days. They'd all been looking forward to eating it that evening, Obāsan in particular. Tomi was at the house, and seeing how big and heavy the fruit was, he offered to carry it. Obāsan politely said she could manage, but Tomi insisted. As he attempted to take it from her hands, it slipped and landed hard upon the ground, exploding into so many pieces that the fleshy fruit splattered to every corner of the room. They did manage to salvage enough of it for everyone to have a piece. But poor Tomi could hardly enjoy his share, which he vehemently tried to refuse, on account of his shame.

Now Hiromu had to find out where Shirō might be and how he might be able to aid him. He prayed that his son was not in a place beyond the realm of help or hope.

"Who is this woman?" Lord Onizuka was in a common area of Yatsushiro Castle when he saw the tax collector, Kasumi, enter. He walked hurriedly with a young woman at his side. He clutched her tightly by one arm with his long bony fingers as he dragged her along.

"She is from one of the villages that failed to pay its tax." Kasumi continued to walk as he spoke. "I am detaining her until payment is rendered."

Onizuka placed himself directly in the tax collector's path, forcing him to a halt. Onizuka looked down at the woman and saw the *suika*-sized bulge of her belly. "Detaining her where?" he asked.

Kasumi regarded the younger man with a look of caution. "I'm taking her to my quarters for the time being, until I decide where to keep her for a longer duration, should that become necessary."

Onizuka smiled from one side of his mouth. "You are quite the pig, aren't you? Are there not enough *geisha* in Yatsushiro to appease your depravity?"

Kasumi's gaunt face shifted into a deformed snarl. "Just whom do you think you're addressing? May I remind you that you are a guest here?"

"A guest?" snapped Onizuka. "Is this some *ryokan* to which I've come to convalesce? I am here by order of Iemitsu Tokugawa, on a mission to burn the churches and eradicate the foreign pestilence that has infected our islands."

"I'm aware of your mission. And I have done my part by enforcing the ancillary taxes on the Christian community. My taking of this woman is within my authority and, as an added benefit, it will aid in the breaking of their spirits. And as long as she's in my custody, I shall take some measure of pleasure for my pains."

"No. I believe I have a more efficient use for this woman."

With that, Onizuka took a hold of Maria's arm and tore it free from Kasumi's skeletal grip.

Maria, whose eyes had been cast down all the while, looked up at Onizuka. Her lovely oval face was swollen and red from crying. She said in a voice barely a whisper, "*Uchi ni kaera sete kudasai.*"*

Onizuka looked upon the woman with affected sympathy. "The hour is late. I shall release you in the morning. You will remain here tonight, but do not fear. You will be given a private quarters." With that, he ordered two of his men to escort her to one of the guest chambers.

Kasumi became indignant. "You have no right! You have no authority over me. I shall report this to Lord Matsui at once."

"Yes, *sukebe*, by all means, report this to Lord Matsui. I have leave from the *shōgun* himself to take whatever measures necessary to carry out my mission. In two days, you will be rid of me as I accompany your Lord Matsui to Kyōto. But tomorrow I shall make a demonstration of the woman."

Kasumi wrung his hands together and leaned in toward the slightly taller man. "If you have no use of her until tomorrow, then at least release her to me tonight."

"Yes, I suppose I could. But I don't care for you, Kasumi. Not for any particular reason. I simply don't like your face. I will not release the woman to you, for no other reason than you desire it."

With that, Kasumi stormed off in search of his master.

---

*"Please, let me go home."

At mid-morning, the banks on either side of the Kuma were lined with crowds of people. It was a Sunday and even with the churches torched and priests imprisoned or deported, it was correctly suspected that many of the Christians in the city would still risk gathering together for communal prayer. It was an uncomplicated task for Onizuka's men, aided by a company of soldiers from the castle, to round up a sizable number of Christians. Many who were corralled railed in protest with shouts of, "*Kirisutokyō de wa nai!*"* But Onizuka was content to snatch them all in his wide net, reasoning he could discourage any would-be converts or sympathizers. In like fashion, on the opposite side of the river, hundreds were forced to march from Sakamoto, known to be a Christian village, to the castle grounds.

The people stood shoulder to shoulder, shivering in the wind that whipped up from the icy waters of the river. Most were lightly clad as they'd been given no opportunity to take a *tanzen* or other garment to protect them from the raw December air. Despite the hour, the sun was hidden behind a low thick quilt of ashen clouds. Most of the trees were bare, having by now shed their foliage, past the point of brilliance.

Onizuka stood upon the long bridge that spanned the river to the castle. The bridge's bright red posts and rails provided the only color to an otherwise bleak scene. With Onizuka stood several of his men, and one woman. Her face, cast down and covered by her long hair, could not be plainly seen. Lying upon the bridge was a long cage-like structure, with coils of thick rope attached to either end, roughly fashioned from stalks of bamboo.

From the direction of the castle, Lord Matsui came

---

*"We are not Christians!"

striding briskly toward them. Even from a distance, the rapid puffs of his breath could be seen rising and dissipating into the air before him. He reached the center of the bridge and panted, "Onizuka-san, is this really necessary?"

Onizuka answered without looking at Matsui. "Perhaps not. But I should think it will have a measurable effect."

"You understand, these people are under my sovereignty. Such a demonstration as this will not endear me to them."

"You may wish to consider the benefits of being feared rather than loved," replied Onizuka. "The *shōgun* would not have dispatched me here had he believed you capable of snuffing out the candle of *kirisutokyō* on your own." Then he turned in the direction of the river and raised his voice so that all along the banks could hear. "Behold this woman! Behold the fate of those who cling to foreign faiths and fail to render what is due!"

With that, Onizuka grabbed a hold of the woman's *yukata* and tore it from her, exposing her naked body and rounded belly. She was then made to lie inside the bamboo cage, as her limbs were tied to its frame. Then the woman named Mariko, who had taken the name Maria upon her baptism, was lowered along with the child in her womb into the frigid flowing waters of the Kuma.

十二

ARRIVAL
到着

*"The more you mow us down, the more numerous
we grow; the blood of Christians is seed."*
Tertullian

*"Seed sinks to the earth
With water, then kiss of sun
new fruits burst to life."*
Masaru

It was nearly dusk when the castle sentries spied the large procession of peasants approaching. Those at the head of the train carried sizable sacks over their shoulders. As the first few among them reached the gate, one of the guards demanded, "What is your business here?"

"We have come to pay our debt," answered a man who was dark complected, with a face that had a look of worn leather.

"Yes, well, that is good, but no scheduled remittance was announced. You must wait here while I inform the tax official."

"Sir, if you please," said the leather-skinned man. "I have

121

carried this sack the entire day's journey. Could you perhaps hold it for me?" Before the guard could answer, the sack was thrust hard into his chest, sending him reeling back and onto the ground. In like manner, the other guards were pummelled with sacks that, unbeknownst to them, were filled not with rice but with large stones. As they lay stunned and injured from the unexpected bludgeoning, they soon found themselves trampled by a peasant army that flooded into the castle like the waters of a burst dam.

The battle that ensued was almost altogether one-sided, as the sparse castle guard was taken utterly unawares. Nearly two-thirds of the castle's force, including Lord Onizuka and his men, had departed that morning to escort Lord Matsui to Kyōto. This intelligence had come to the villagers through Shirō upon his return to Takazawa. He had borne with him as well the news of the execution of Yoshimura's wife and unborn child. He, along with hundreds of others, had witnessed the execrable act from the river bank.

The grief and revulsion he felt at the sight of the brutal deed was only amplified by the torment of helplessness. He had travelled to Yatsushiro with the singular hope of negotiating the woman's release. And he had offered up fervent prayers of petition for success the entire half-day journey from Takazawa. But as he watched with horror as the woman's body slowly slipped into the icy waters, he felt the familiar emptiness of despair. And for the first time in his young life, he felt even some measure of anger directed toward the One to whom his prayers had been offered. But once the news of Maria reached her village, any reservations about rebellion were consumed by the anger channeled toward Yatsushiro.

The men of the castle guard attempted to stand their ground, bringing down several of the attackers beneath their blades. But the sheer number of the peasants, with many *rōnin* among their ranks, was too great for the skeleton crew guard to overcome. Though far less skilled in the fighting arts, the assailants charged with alarming rabidity. While the *rōnin* carried shorter blades and three-pronged *sai* that had been easily concealed, most of the intruders wielded hoes, pitchforks, and every sort of farming implement they could muster from the villages. In a matter of mere minutes, the guards who remained standing found themselves, as they waved their swords before them in distress, pinned with their backs against stone walls and wooden pillars.

From the moment he set foot inside the fortress, Yoshimura ran about like a wild animal with a singular purpose. He made his way down the length of the central corridor, methodically peeking into every room and alcove, ploughing through any object or body that obstructed his progress. When he reached the end of the corridor, he came to one last room and kicked through its thin sliding door of wood and paper. Curled up in the far corner of the room sat Kasumi, the tax collector. He sat bolt upright upon Yoshimura's explosive entry. He squinted as though to make certain he was not seeing some phantasm. But his eyes widened as a look of recognition came over his face. He began to stammer, "Now, don't be rash. I was not responsible for her death. It was on Lord Onizuka's orders—not mine!"

Yoshimura raised the long pitchfork he carried, and pointed its tines toward the tax collector's face. He spoke with an anger that was palpable yet controlled. "You took her from me."

Kasumi's voice was oily, yet he could not conceal the fear in his eyes. He glanced toward the splintered doorway and out into the corridor, in the hopeful expectancy of aid that was not forthcoming. "You don't want my blood on your hands. You know what the penalty would be for the murder of an official." Kasumi slowly stood up, his back sliding against the wall. "Besides, you are a Christian. Your own religion commands that you forgive your enemies."

Yoshimura took one step toward the collector, the fork still raised in his trembling hands. "The fortress is taken. Our lives are already forfeit. You may believe we have come here for vengeance. That was reason enough for me to seek you out. But this place has been stormed because the people starve. Yes, my religion commands that I pray for my enemies." Yoshimura held the long fork with his left hand while he made a sign of the cross with his right. "And I shall pray for mercy upon your soul." With those words, he thrust the tines of the fork deep into the tax collector's abdomen. He stared directly into the wide surprised eyes of his victim, and then pulled the tool sharply back to himself. Kasumi stood there, his hands pressed against the puncture wounds, and cast a pleading look toward his executioner.

Yoshimura whispered to himself, "Just as I will pray for mercy upon my own." He once again raised the tool, normally used for the gathering of straw and leaves, and thrust it into Kasumi's throat. The center tine pierced through the soft flesh just below the larynx, while the two outer tines went around the man's neck and into the wall behind him. Yoshimura turned away and walked out of the room, leaving the body of the tax collector pinned against the wall like an insect fastened to a display board.

Back in the corridor, the fighting had begun to subside. The sounds of clashing wood and steel gave way to the duller sounds of weapons falling to the floor. The invading force had outnumbered the castle guard, caught completely by surprise, by nearly twelve to one. Several of the peasant fighters had fallen, though surprisingly few. Their success, as one of the *rōnin* would later note, was not so much due to their fighting skills as an understanding that hesitation in the moment of battle was not an option. And they had not hesitated. More than half the castle forces lay dead or wounded, while the rest had been driven back to the large chamber room where Shirō had met with Lord Matsui just two days before. The defeated defenders now found themselves pressed against the walls of the chamber as the intruders kept their weapons drawn and pointed toward them.

Shirō was the one who spoke to address them. "We did not come here solely seeking bloodshed. But the restoration of justice and honor demanded the taking of this place."

One of the castle soldiers, a captain, stepped forward. "You have all sealed your own warrants of execution. Do you think this act of insurrection could go unpunished? You will all be hunted down and put to slow deaths."

Shirō answered, "There will be no need to hunt us down, for we will remain here." He turned his attention away from the captain and addressed the whole of the castle guard. "I believe there may be those among you sympathetic to the plight of the people, those of you who know the cruelties of your masters to be unlawful. We have come not for the obliteration of order, but for its restoration. Any of you who wish to remain will be welcomed. Otherwise you are at liberty to leave."

There was murmuring among the castle soldiers and, for a few tense moments, it seemed as though some might make an attempt to regain control. But the only weapons within reach were the ones poised and ready to strike them. The peasant army slowly backed away enough to form an alley through which the guards were permitted to retreat and exit the castle. Nearly all of them departed, their heads cast toward the ground. But about thirty remained. One of them was the guard that Shirō thought he had recognized when he'd arrived at the castle two days earlier.

In the hours that followed, many more from villages throughout the region poured into the fortress—men, women, and children to the number of about five thousand. They came in anger over the abuses, and in the hope of turning political tides, but mostly they came because they were hungry.

十三

News Comes to Kyōto
京都に知らせが来る

*"The Queen of the South will rise up with the men
of this generation at the judgment and condemn them,
because she came from the ends of the earth to hear
the wisdom of Solomon. And behold, something
greater than Solomon is here."*
Luke 11:31

*"No art of learning is to be pursued half-heartedly …
and any art worth learning will certainly reward more
or less generously the effort made to study it."*
Murasaki Shikibu, The Tale of Genji

The *daimyō* of the southern regions sat in the great hall of Nijō Castle. The flatland stronghold, the grounds of which sprawled over twenty-seven *chōbu*, had been built by Ieyasu Tokugawa, grandfather of the new *shōgun*, Iemitsu. The man who bridged the generations, Hidetada, had been laid to rest the previous day. After his body had been publicly cremated upon the funeral pyre, family members formed the traditional line for the *kotsuage*, the collecting of bone remnants. During the ritual, the pieces of bone not incinerated by the fires were passed, using long wooden *hashi*, from one relative to the next, and then deposited into an urn along with the ashes. This, of course, was the only occasion on which passing something from hashi to hashi was permissible.

Iemitsu bowed formally to his sister, Masako, as he placed the glossy glazed ceramic urn into her hands. Upon it was painted the *aoi no gomon*—the three leaves of hollyhock in a circle—the Tokugawa family crest. Hidetada's remains were to be interred at Zōjō-ji temple, beside the shrine dedicated to Minamoto Yoritomo, the empire's first *shōgun* from four-and-a-half centuries earlier.

Some fifteen years ago, Hidetada had artfully arranged the marriage of his daughter, Masako, to the emperor. It was a most logical tactic to exercise influence if not complete control over a monarch who, though still revered by the people as a deity, was politically little more than a figurehead. There were, however, occasions on which his imperial son-in-law, Go-Mizuno, acted in ways that caused friction.

On one such recent occasion, Go-Mizuno, a staunch supporter of the Zen Buddhists, had granted special permission for the monks of Daitoku and Myōshin temples to wear imperially-sanctioned purple robes, a sign of high ranking and the emperor's favor. This did not sit well with the elder Tokugawa, as the monks were becoming increasingly vocal in their criticism of the feudal system. Indeed, Hidetada's father, Ieyasu Tokugawa, was forced to deal harshly with one particular sect of warrior monks who had incited uprisings in opposition to *samurai* rule. Hidetada usurped the emperor's authority by prohibiting the wearing of the purple robes. Some of the monks who resisted the ban were exiled to the cold remote provinces of the north. Hidetada would have gladly had them executed, but decided such a move might rouse the sympathy of the commoners. By his actions, Hidetada had demonstrated his resolve to exercise authority in religious as well as temporal matters.

The incident was seen by the emperor as a matter of personal dishonor, and it was perhaps for this reason that he chose to save face by his abdication. Now his daughter Meishō, just barely thirteen years of age, was the incumbent monarch of the empire. It was rumored that she had a curiosity about the religion of the Spanish and Portuguese missionaries. On one occasion, she summoned a Catholic priest to the palace to ask him all manner of questions about the faith and the god-man they called Iesu. She was also quite keen to learn about the mother of Iesu. Meishō found fascinating the belief that the one named Maria was revered as the queen of heaven, and spiritual mother of the whole human race.

Iemitsu was incensed when he learned of the encounter. It may have provided the spark that ignited his campaign to rid the country of the missionaries. Indeed, it may even have been a contributing factor that prompted the arrest and public execution of twenty-six Christians in Nagasaki.

Iemitsu Tokugawa, newly appointed *shōgun* and uncle of the empress, looked out upon the *daimyō* gathered in the hall. Though relatively small in stature, the imposing nature of his physical presence was palpable. A face that might otherwise have been quite pleasant was drawn into an almost perpetual scowl, like a *bunraku* puppet donning the mask of a villainous character. His eyes were wide and steely, with dark circles below them and knitted brows above. His jowls were noticeably pronounced for a man not even of middle age, and one could imagine how much more so they would someday become. In his suit of leather armor and round *jingasa* hat with its domed peak, he looked just as much the part of a military general as did his father and grandfather, perhaps even more so.

There had been several orders of business, the most pressing of which was the expulsion of the Iberian merchants and missionaries. Several of the *daimyō* expressed their concerns about what impact this would have on trade and all its profitable advantages, not to mention the acquisition of firearms and other instruments of warfare. But Tokugawa assured them that another potentially more powerful allegiance was being forged. The Dutch East India Company was establishing itself in the Asian mainland and was quite eager to expand its commercial dealings to the Japanese islands.

But this time, Iemitsu would be sure not to make the same mistake as his predecessors in allowing the foreigners to spread their religious propaganda. Indeed, the Dutch expressed no desire to do so. Theirs was a different sect of Christianity, one that renounced the authority of the leader in Rome. Their interests appeared to be purely economic. In any event, Tokugawa would take the necessary steps to ensure the *gaijin* would have minimal contact with the general populace.

As the meeting was coming to a close, a messenger entered the room as swiftly as he could without disturbing the air of formality. He was perspiring profusely and was short of breath. "*Tono*, I beg your pardon, but there is urgent news from Yatsushiro."

Tokugawa looked up at the messenger, who was frozen in

a deep bow and awaiting permission to speak. With a slight nod and short grunt, Tokugawa granted permission. Lord Matsui, who was sitting to his left, had spun quickly upon hearing the mention of Yatsushiro.

"*Tono*, an army of farmers has attacked and now occupies the castle grounds."

Matsui's mouth opened, though he dared not speak. Tokugawa stood abruptly, as though something had stung him. He looked at Matsui and then back to the messenger.

"It occurred three days ago, *Tono*. They arrived under the pretense of delivering their due taxes. They gained entry and seized control."

Tokugawa was holding a fan in his right hand, and he swatted it at the air as if trying to kill whatever had stung him. "How many?" he demanded.

"It's uncertain. The reports suggest several hundred, perhaps over a thousand."

Tokugawa turned to Matsui. "How many men did you leave at the castle?"

Matsui appeared flummoxed. Only a short time before, he'd been enjoying a hot cup of *matcha* tea, and the hope of currying more favored status with Tokugawa. Now he suddenly felt like a dog whose excrement had been discovered somewhere in the master's house. He began to stammer, "*Anō...eeto...*"

"Never mind!" bellowed Tokugawa, "Perhaps you required fewer men to protect your body on the journey here, and more to guard your domicile!"

The messenger, still bowing with his eyes cast downward, spoke again, "*Tono*, General Hosokawa in Kumamoto is aware of the situation. He has troops assembled and ready to take back the castle."

Tokugawa turned again to Matsui. "You had better get

back and handle affairs. I still expect all that we discussed today to be carried out in full measure."

Matsui, having only arrived in Kyōto that very morning, was still weary from the journey. He had hoped to enjoy some of the carnal pleasures of the city, certainly the company of at least one *geisha*. But he knew far better than to voice any complaint.

十四

UNDER SIEGE
攻撃を受ける

*"Humiliation followeth the proud, and glory shall uphold
the humble of spirit."*
Proverbs 29:23

"Even monkeys fall from trees."
Japanese proverb

"Master Shirō, an army approaches from the north." The
scout was laboring to breathe as he panted out the
words.

"How many?" Shirō stood upon the walkway along the
parapet of the fortress's central outer wall. With him were
Tomi, Hashizume, and several of the other *rōnin* leaders from
the various villages. They were discussing what their options
might be, all the while keeping watch for the inevitable
arrival of forces who would attempt to retake the castle.

"Three thousand strong."

When news of the insurrection reached Kumamoto
Castle, General Hosokawa did not wait to receive orders
from Kyōto. Five years earlier, he had been given control over

133

Kumamoto Castle and the entire Higo province that made up a large portion of Kyūshū. Of particular importance were the ports of Yatsushiro, Nagasaki, and Amakusa, where the first missionaries had arrived decades earlier.

Hosokawa had been appointed by Hidetada Tokugawa to replace Lord Kato, the castle's previous master. Kato had been much beloved amongst all the classes—peasants, merchants, and *samurai* alike. Kato's mother had actually been the cousin of the first Tokugawa *shōgun*, Ieyasu. Kato was an ardent lover of nature, as well as a student of engineering. It was he who oversaw the construction of Kumamoto Castle, as well as many projects to ensure the longevity of the region's forests, and the building of irrigation systems that significantly increased the annual yields of rice.

But Hidetada perceived that Kato was too much loved and not enough feared. He had been more than accommodating in allowing the Jesuit missionaries to build their churches and evangelize the people. Converts were numbering into the thousands, and young Japanese men were even beginning to be ordained as priests. When Tokugawa learned of rumors that Kato himself might have secretly become a Christian, that was the final straw. Hosokawa, who had a reputation for knowing how to keep the peasant class in line, was moved from his position in the far north of Kyūshū to Kumamoto.

General Hosokawa knew that whatever the contributing factors to the insurrection, the first order of business was to take back the fortress at Yatsushiro. The general quickly gathered his own force of about five hundred *samurai*. Other *daimyō* in the region, upon learning that the uprising was a disgruntled band of peasants, were not terribly enthusiastic about getting involved. There was, after all, little glory to be gained by the slaughter of a band of farmers wielding hoes and spades.

But this changed when it became known that there were many *rōnin*, particularly Christians, amongst the peasants. Now this became a chance to secure favor with the new *shōgun*, with the added benefit of giving their own *samurai* an opportunity to put their sharply honed skills and swords to some practical use. Though some of the elder ones had fought at Sekigahara, a few even at the siege of Ōsaka, and some even in the invasions of Joseon Korea during the Imjin Wars, many of the junior men were not battle-hardened.

Without invitation, the *daimyō* reported to Kumamoto Castle under their respective banners to offer their services. General Hosokawa, while privately preferring to handle the matter on his own, nonetheless accepted the aid so as not to offend any senses of honor. And so, on a cold January afternoon, just a week after the Christians celebrated the birth of their Messiah, six armies numbering three thousand men in total, arrived to take back possession of the partially restored ruins of Yatsushiro Castle.

Shirō and the others watched as the army approached. From the frost covered ground came the advancing soft crunch of thousands of feet and hooves. The men on horseback were at the front of the procession which, as it drew nearer, spread out to form a line that surrounded the walls of the fortress—all but the one wall that faced the sea. The riders were most splendidly arrayed in their finest armor. One of them in particular caught the attention of Tomi, who began to point excitedly. "Shirō, do you see that rider in the crimson armor?"

Shirō looked and immediately spotted the man, most noble in his posture, wearing an armor suit of blood-red leather.

"Yes, I see him," replied Shirō. Then, with a flicker of recognition he added, "Wait, is he who I think he is?"

"I am quite certain of it!" Tomi's expression, normally serious or sardonic, now exhibited an uncharacteristic childlike glee.

The rider was none other than Tomi's longtime idol, the legendary Miyamoto Musashi himself. Master Musashi had been a long-term guest at Kumamoto Castle, where he spent his days training and teaching the art of advanced swordsmanship to the castle guard. He had been asked by Hosokawa to come this day in an advisory capacity, and Musashi was not one to turn down an opportunity to put his tactical principles into practice.

Musashi had advised Hosokawa, "My suggestion is that we hold down the pillow." "Holding down the pillow," a term Musashi had coined in his book, was a way to describe the act of not allowing one's enemy to dictate the course of action. While an opponent is in a static position, the key is to strike before he has the opportunity to move. "Now that they have contained themselves within the confines of the fortress, you must strike swiftly."

General Hosokawa had asked Musashi, on account of his esteemed status, to act as mouthpiece to address those within the fortress walls. Musashi was initially reluctant, but did finally oblige. He rode forward to a vantage point where he could clearly be seen by those standing upon the parapet. Tomi was awestruck at the sight of this regal figure about whom he knew so much, but had never before seen in the flesh. Musashi's even and authoritative voice rose up, amplified as it echoed against the stone walls of the fortress.

"Farmers and warriors of Higo—I understand that you have cause for your discontent! But the taking of life and property constitutes a criminal, and in this case even treasonous act! You have embarked upon a path that can lead only to your own demise! But it is not too late to veer from that path! I have been assured that if you surrender yourselves peaceably, your lives will be spared!"

As Musashi was delivering this address, Yoshimura arrived upon the parapet. He held in his hand a bronze chamber pot discovered amongst some of the rubble within the fortress. He had brought it up to add to the collection of heavy objects gathered over the past several days, though someone had suggested that it might be better to put it to its intended use. In Yoshimura's eyes were flames of fury further fueled by every word that bellowed up from the mouth of the master swordsman.

Tightly grasping its handle, Yoshimura raised the pot above his head and shouted down, "Here is your answer!" With that, he threw the object down with such power and precision that it struck Musashi squarely on the left side of his head. The forceful impact knocked him from his horse, and he landed hard with his right shoulder upon the frosty ground.

Some men ran to his aid, but he waved them off. "*Daijōbu yo!*" he repeated several times as he got back onto his feet. He dusted himself off and gave his head a good shake. Then he let out a long laugh. "Well, I believe if they've already resorted to throwing anything they can lay hands upon, you haven't too much to fear." Then, turning to General Hosokawa, he said, "I leave this matter in your capable hands." And with that he remounted his horse and made his exit from the scene. While still within earshot, he turned and added, "Just don't underestimate their fighting spirit!"

Shirō, Tomi, and the others upon the parapet stood and watched the legendary swordsman ride off as the full circle of the red sun began its descent over the waters of the bay. Tomi looked forlorn. "What's wrong?" asked Shirō "We should be grateful to see such a potential adversary turning away!"

Tomi looked away from the sight of Musashi's slowly disappearing figure and toward the setting sun. "I just witnessed my hero knocked from his horse by a peasant's chamber pot."

十五

PROPHECY
預言

*"Blessed be the Lord my strength, who trains my hands
for war and teaches my fingers to fight."*
Psalm 144

*"The finest of flowers is the cherry blossom—
of men, the warrior."*
Japanese proverb

"Bring the *hashigo!*" General Hosokawa gave the order and immediately those in the front lines gave way to allow men from behind to come forward. They came running up in teams carrying long ladders of bamboo above their heads—sturdy yet light and easy to wield. About twenty ladders were leaned against each of the fortress's three land-facing walls. Care was taken to place the ladders at such an angle so that they reached the tops of the walls without extending beyond, lest the defenders simply push them away. As this was taking place, no one could be seen any longer upon the parapet. Still, Hosokawa carefully scanned the top of the wall for any figure raising itself. He did not wish to become the next

139

recipient of another chamber pot projectile.

Like an army of ants, soldiers began to scurry deftly up the rungs. Swords in their scabbards swung and clanked as they struck the hollow sides of the bamboo ladders. Below, additional lines of men waited poised and ready to ascend as soon as the first wave made it up and over the other side of the wall.

Within the walls, unseen by those outside, men waited upon a lower parapet, exactly halfway up the walls. They kept close watch through holes just wide enough to allow for an unobstructed view to the outside. As the first of the would-be invaders reached the level of those holes, the men inside gave a loud shout, "*Sei.....no!*"

With this signal, those along the upper parapet sprang into action. Within the fortress walls was an abundance of materials meant for the ongoing construction and renovations. In the days before the arrival of the army from Kumamoto, the peasants had hoisted lengths of timber, large landscaping stones, and even a life-size bronze statue of the meditating Buddha, to the upper parapet. Now the men raised themselves up, some on their own, others with a companion, wielding the weighty objects and hurling them down the outer side of the wall.

Shirō and Tomi squatted at either end of a thick wooden pole the length of two men. They'd been watching each other, waiting for the moment to act. Tomi said to Shirō, "I hope you're strong enough to manage your end, you runt!"

Shirō smiled and answered, "Just be sure not to throw yourself over!" They lifted the pole in balanced unison and released it over the top of the wall. The hefty thing plummeted quickly, settled into the curve of the wall, and rolled straight into the chest of the top man on a ladder below. The man's sternum and ribs cracked as he was hurtled down along with the pole, taking out several men on the ladder below him. In like fashion, all those upon the parapet, including women and even some of the older children, unleashed a hail storm of poles and heavy stones. As one poor fellow looked up from his position on a ladder, the last thing he saw in this life was the head of a Buddha statue that, as it struck his own head, split it open like an overly ripened melon.

When the barrage finally ended, splintered ladders and broken bodies lay strewn along the perimeter of the castle.

During the week before the first attack was repelled, those within the sanctuary of the fortress walls had celebrated the birth of their Savior. As Shirō gazed up into the night sky on the eve of that day, it appeared to him that the very stars danced, and the entire universe echoed with a music that, if human ears could perceive it, might cause the hearer to die from its overwhelming beauty.

Unbeknownst to the *shōgun* in Kyōto or anyone else outside the region, thousands more had poured into the grounds of the old citadel in the days that followed its takeover by an army of disenchanted peasants and their *rōnin* captains. When word of the castle's occupation spread, so did other uprisings. Abuses had simply become too grievous and frequent to bear. With no other discernible recourse, villages throughout the region, and even in nearby Amakusa, were taking up arms against local authorities. The commoners had been pushed beyond the boundaries of sufferance with the imposition of the *fumie*. And they were hungry. Seeking food and what they hoped would be safety in numbers, they made their way to Yatsushiro in droves.

After the takeover of the castle, the rebels had discovered massive warehouses where rice and other grains, along with a wide variety of vegetables, dried fish, and other foodstuffs had been hoarded. It was far more than all of Matsui's *samurai* could have consumed over any reasonable period of time. The sight of so much food was at once a cause for both relief and rage. They knew there was plenty to meet the needs of the numbers who had arrived, but not indefinitely. And so a plan was immediately put in place to ration the provisions. Each morning, the people reported to designated stations within the expansive grounds, where they were given rice and other foods according to the numbers within their families.

But *Natāru*, as they called it using the Portuguese—a word that also meant "birth,"—was a feast day, and provisions were handed out rather more freely. There had been several head of cattle within the fortress grounds, and those trained in the art of butchery oversaw the task of preparing the animals for consumption. For many, it was the first time to sample the simple yet succulent dish of *gyūdon*, a bowl of rice topped with tender cooked beef and onions.

The one thing for which the people wanted, even more acutely on this day, was the presence of a priest. Though they lamented their inability to celebrate the *Misa*, still they did all they could to faithfully signify a humble gratitude for the infant king born to a young virgin, at the time when Suinin was only the eleventh emperor of their islands.

In years past, the eve of *Natāru* was marked by lengthy readings from the Sacred Scriptures. The first part of the evening was devoted to the stories of the old covenants and prophecies of the Messiah whose coming had been long foretold. This was followed late into the night with the accounts of the life of Iesu himself, and the fulfillment of all the prophecies. Over time, many of the stories came to be acted out by talented amateurs and trained artists alike in the form of plays. And there, within the stone sentinel walls of the fortress, the people were moved nearly to tears as an actor angel escorted the first man and woman out of the garden of paradise. But consolation would arrive when that same angel announced news of a distant day of salvation.

And then there was the exchange of gifts. The early Jesuit missionaries had observed, with no small degree of astonishment, the way in which the natives, without any prompting beyond hearing the story of the three Magi, had applied the act of gift-giving—something so natural to them—to the celebration of *Natāru*. Even under the circumstances in which they now found themselves, the elders had the time and materials to make simple toys for the hundreds of children who had arrived with their families at the castle grounds. In the open courtyards, the laughter of the young ones could be heard as they ran about wielding hand-fashioned *kendama*,* and twirling *taketombo*† into the cold late December air.

Shirō watched the children at play. He joined in with them and for a while forgot about the turmoil and threat of retaliation outside the false sense of security the walls offered. He watched the children and his heart became suddenly filled with a yearning to return to his own childhood. He longed to see his mother and father—and Kumiko. *The holy family*, he thought, *suffered through trying conditions on this night so many years ago, but at least they were together.*

---

*Literally, "sword and ball," a skill toy consisting of a wooden handle with a cup at its end into which one tries to catch a wooden ball on a string.
†Literally, "bamboo dragonfly," a toy consisting of a thin dowel attached to a bamboo shaving propeller. It takes flight when the user spins the dowel between the palms of the hands.

A voice interrupted his thoughts. "Nakagawa-san, some of us would like a word with you." It was Hashizume. With him was the castle guard that Shirō had recognized the day he first arrived to speak to Matsui and seek the release of Yoshimura's wife. Shirō had spoken to the guard following the taking of the fortress. He learned that the young man, whose name was Uemura, had studied at the seminary on Amakusa at the time Shirō was there studying medicine. They had attended *Misa* together on at least one occasion. "Please," continued Hashizume, "come with us."

Uemura led Shirō to the northwest corner of the fortress, far from where any crowds were gathered. Several of the *rōnin* and other men were standing along the western wall that faced the sea. Many of them had serious expressions, though some smiled when Shirō arrived. After greeting them all with a bow, he said, "I assume there is something you do not wish the people to hear."

"Quite the contrary," replied Hashizume. "There is something we do wish for the people to hear. But we wanted you to hear it first. We will allow Uemura-san to explain."

Uemura was a handsome man of medium build, and about seven years Shirō's senior. He had a deep and silky voice that was pleasant to the ear. He began to convey to Shirō what he had told the others several hours earlier. "When I was in Amakusa, one of the Jesuits told to me a tale of one of the first missionaries to arrive in the time of our great-grandparents. He was a mystic and a visionary. Among other things, he spoke of a time when there would be a great persecution of those who professed the *fukuin*, the Gospel of Our Blessed Lord."

Shirō nodded. "Iesu himself told his disciples that the world would despise them, just as it had despised him first. We have always known that to follow Our Lord means to carry the cross."

"Please, Nakagawa-san, hear all that Uemura-san has to say." It was the voice of Hashizume.

"*Sumimasen*," said Shirō as he bowed in apology.

Uemura continued. "The priest, whose name is now uncertain, spoke of a time when a young man would rise up to lead the people against their oppressors. This man would be healer as well as warrior. And this time would be marked by signs. As the prophecy states, 'The skies will be the color of vermilion, and flowers will blossom out of season.'"

This time, Shirō waited for sufficient pause to speak. "It is an interesting tale. But why have you summoned me here to share it?"

Hashizume placed his hands upon Shirō's shoulders. "Nakagawa-san, look up at the skies. Have you not noticed their color these days since we've arrived here?"

"*Hai*," replied Shirō. "They have reminded me of the morning skies of early autumn. Many hours did I spend as a child staring up into such skies from the hillsides of Watari."

"There is something else we wish for you to see," said Hashizume. With that, they led Shirō around the corner of a small potting shed. Behind it was a solitary cherry blossom tree that looked to be perhaps a few years in age. It was, quite astonishingly, in full bloom.

Uemura spoke. "Shirō-san, many of us believe we are witnessing the signs of the prophecy. We also believe that you may be the one whose coming was foretold."

Shirō laughed aloud. "I confess I am astounded to see this tree displaying such lovely pink petals in this month. Indeed, I am daily amazed by God's creation. But I will not entertain the notion that I, nor any one among us for that matter, is some messiah. We celebrate the birth of the one true Savior

145

this day. It is upon Him that our hearts and wills must be focused."

Uemura spoke again, this time with greater urgency. "Shirō-san, I believe the one who gave the prophecy was in earnest. I further believe that the people desperately desire a leader. If we make a public proclamation that you are the one whose coming was foretold, it will give them hope, and something real to rally behind. For their sake, accept this mantle placed before you."

Shirō looked upon the blossoms of the cherry tree, and then up to the crimson horizon. He spoke softly while he still gazed upward. "The one who gave this prophecy of which you speak—he may well have been in earnest. Yet this is not part of the deposit of faith. I am neither a leader nor a hero. One night, I followed a shadow into the woods, and the course of my life was changed. The next day, I set out to rescue a friend. And now here we are, awaiting a fate uncertain to us but known to God. It is He in whom we place our trust. There will be no proclamation, public or otherwise, that I am anything other than what I am—a Christian warrior who will do what he may to serve our Lord and my neighbor."

With that, Shirō gently bowed to the men and departed back to the courtyards and the people. Respecting Shirō's wish, no public proclamation regarding the prophecy was ever made. Word of it, however, did circulate among the people. And, for reasons no one would ever quite know for certain, word of the prophecy and the name of Shirō Nakagawa reached even to the ears of Iemitsu Tokugawa in Kyōto, as well as the Empress Meishō in Edo.

十六

SECOND WAVE
第二波

*"It is mine to avenge; I will repay. In due time their foot
will slip; their day of disaster is near and their doom
rushes upon them."*
Deuteronomy 32:35

"If you would avenge yourself, dig two graves."
Japanese proverb

The light of the *mikazuki* crescent moon, aided by the
flickering glow of their torches, allowed the soldiers to
see a sufficient distance. The walls of the castle were dimly
illumined, as disfigured shadows appearing like hunched
ogres were cast upon them. Ladders leaned askew against
the walls, and patches of blood glistened in the moonlight.
With the river at their backs, General Hosokawa conferred
with his captains about the next line of attack.

They decided that they would once again line the walls
with ladders. But this time, they would stagger the attack,
ascending in irregular intervals to make themselves less easy
targets. Archers, freshly arrived from Kumamoto, would

stand at the ready to deliver a suppressing volley at the first sight of so much as the top of a head or tip of a finger upon the wall. As Hosokawa was conveying his orders, one of the captains appeared distracted. Hosokawa snapped, "*Chanto kīte iru no?* Are you listening?"

The captain's face had a look of concerted concentration. "*Taishō*, do you hear that?" Hosokawa intuitively tilted his head in the same direction as the captain's. He could indeed hear something. It was faint and distant, but it was clearly human. And it was clearly female.

Hosokawa shouted, "*Shizuka ni!*" and everyone in the camp fell silent. The sound, now a discernible rhythmic pulse, was coming from the direction of the forest to the east.

"Aaa…iii…aaa…" The sound grew increasingly louder and more insistent.

Within the fortress walls, Shirō and Tomi looked at one another with puzzled expressions. They, along with all those standing upon the parapet, could also hear what sounded like chanting in the distance. "Aaa…iii…aaa…" It continued for several minutes.

Tomi's eyes widened and he said, as though to himself, "They're saying 'Maria.'"

And they all recognized it as the chanting became clearer. "Maa…rii..aa…" It was the name of The Blessed Mother. And it was the name of Yoshimura's wife who was drowned, together with the child in her womb, in the frigid waters of the Kuma.

Hosokawa became agitated over the strange intrusion. He ordered one of the captains to take a squad of men to investigate its source. By the pale light of the moon, amplified by their torches, the soldiers could make out the edge of the bamboo grove from which the chanting was emanating, but they could see no one. They stood waving their torches at the forest edge as the sound continued to grow louder. Some of the men appeared frightened, as though the voices might be coming from spirits in the forest or from the very trees themselves.

Shadows began to emerge from the grove. And then the shadows took on recognizable form. A long line of at least a hundred women spanned the edge of the grove as far as the eye could see. Their chanting continued and intensified. The soldiers stood and stared, unsure of how to react. The captain finally called out, "This is the site of a military operation! You must vacate at once!"

The chanting only grew louder.

The captain had enough. He ordered the men, "Detain these women, and take them down to the river!" The soldiers advanced, one of them seizing a woman by her wrist. In an instant, she produced a small knife from the folds of her *yukata*, and plunged it into the soldier's hip. With a perplexed look on his face, he squeezed the wrist in his hand all the more tightly. Then he saw a quick flash of something spring from out of the grove. A moment later, he realized he no longer had a hold of the woman, because his own hand had fallen to the ground. He sank to his knees, eyes wide with shock. The pain would come shortly after.

As the maimed soldier fell, a long line of men dressed in dark armor emerged from the cover of the grove, deftly weaving their way through the spaces between the women. They wielded swords and made short shrift of the soldiers from Kumamoto. One of the men in black raised his left hand and gave a shout. He and the others ran forward in the direction of the castle. As they did, hundreds more emerged like a swarm from the forest.

At the fortress perimeter, General Hosokawa noticed the chanting had ceased, and he awaited a report of what had transpired. He also noticed something else, something that didn't seem quite right. The light of the torches his men had been carrying no longer formed a single line at the edge of the distant grove. They now appeared scattered, many even extinguished. As he strained to see more clearly, a dark wave rose up from the bottom of the hill that separated the fortress grounds from the edge of the wood. By the muted light of the pallid moon, the wave had a low sheen, like a black silk curtain in a candlelit room. The general sat atop his horse and stared, as though mesmerized by the hypnotic effect, until he finally realized what he was seeing.

Hosokawa raised his sword with his right hand, as he shouted for his men to take up arms. An invisible force pushed his arm back with a violent jolt. He looked and saw that the hilt of his sword had been replaced by the notched end of an arrow that had pierced his hand. The air became filled with the hissing of arrows, many of which found a target of bone and flesh.

The black army soon entered into the camp and commenced a hand-to-hand fight. The shrill ring of clashing steel pierced through the biting air as the defenders, the river to their backs, attempted to hold their ground. From within the fortress walls, Shirō and the others looked down upon the scene. Tomi shouted above the din, "Who are they?"

"I'm not sure," answered Shirō, "but it certainly appears they've come to our aid." They continued to observe from their high vantage point upon the parapet and could see the battle was far from over. The soldiers of Kumamoto, though initially taken unawares, had now regrouped and, with their superior numbers, were beginning to push back the mysterious invaders.

"Shirō!" It was the voice of Hashizume. "Yet more are approaching!" He pointed to the northeast and, as they looked into the distance, they could see another large force of men running from the woods toward the fortress. These men wore armor like that of *samurai* but with cords of large beads around their necks. Over their heads and faces were white coverings, and in their hands they wielded long staffs and *naginata*.

"They are *sōhei*," uttered Tomi, with a tone of awe.

"*Sōhei?*" asked Shirō. "Are you sure?"

"Yes, he is right," confirmed Hashizume.

The *sōhei* were Buddhist monk warriors, many of whom had been mercenaries or criminals, some even former *samurai*, before seeking lives of peaceful contemplation. Over time, many of the various Buddhist sects had become increasingly open in their opposition to feudal rule. In response, the *daimyō* Oda Nobunaga, waged a campaign against these sects some half century earlier. Temples were razed and their occupants imprisoned or executed. Many of those who managed to escape formed militia-like companies that roamed the countryside. During the Sengoku period of internal warring, it was known that the services of the *sōhei* could often be bought by the highest bidding *daimyō* in his rivalry against another. Though armed clashes with *samurai* were now rare, the legendary aura of the *sōhei* yet remained.

"They must have been hired to assist the army from Kumamoto," said Tomi. Since the arrival of the missionaries, there had been ongoing tension, even hostility, between the Christian converts and the Buddhists.

Hashizume added, "They may well have been pleased to volunteer their services for the opportunity to help rid the island of a rival religion."

Shirō replied, "We must get outside and join with those who have come to help us."

Tomi's expression became grave. "Shirō, if you send out

these farmer fighters, the *sōhei* will mow them down like so many stalks of dry bamboo."

But Shirō answered, "I'm not going to stand here while those who came to our aid perish from our lack of reciprocation."

Hashizume spoke, "The experienced among us will go out to meet them."

Men from the fortress descended quickly down the ladders still leaning against the walls, while others poured out through the narrow *uzumimon* gate in the wall that faced the bay. Running in the direction of the northeast wood, they formed a line to cut off the fast approaching *sōhei*. As Shirō and the others braced themselves for the impending collision, he saw in his mind's eye an image of the brute who had rushed upon him that fateful night in the church. He felt fear, but recalled the words of one of the fighting instructors from his youth. "When anticipating an attack, be at once both excited and relaxed. Focus on breathing, the source of life, and doing whatever is required to sustain it."

As the *sōhei* came within throwing distance, Shirō could see only their eyes through the wrappings that covered the rest of their faces. He said a silent prayer, "Lord, help me to be swift and strong. Yet, not my will but yours be done." He and the others raised their swords.

The *sōhei* abruptly stopped in their tracks. With their weapons at their sides, they turned their heads toward one among them who appeared to be the leader. This man took one small step back and offered a deep bow to Shirō and his companions. The rest of the *sōhei* did likewise.

Shirō and his companions looked at one another with perplexed expressions. The *sōhei* leader spoke: "We've come to fight with you, not against you."

"But why?" asked Shirō.

"We know the pain of persecution. We also know that there

are women and children in this keep." The leader then stretched his neck to see beyond the line of Shirō and the others. "There will be time to talk later. For now, allow us to pass!"

For a moment, Shirō wondered if this could be some sort of ruse. But then he reasoned that if these men wanted to kill Christians, they could begin with the ones standing right before them. Addressing the leader, Shirō said, "You shall not pass, but rather join us." With that, he and the others from the fortress turned in the opposite direction. Together with the *sōhei*, they ran toward the river to face the soldiers from Kumamoto. The words Tomi had spoken earlier turned out to be prophetic, as the *sōhei* cut through their opponents like so many stalks of dry bamboo.

The soldiers from Kumamoto, wedged between the two unexpected forces, soon found themselves in an impossible situation. When the fighting ceased, fewer than a hundred of Hosokawa's men, including the general himself, stood pinned against the southern wall of the fortress.

Shirō was the one to step forward and address them. "Soldiers of Kumamoto, leave with your swords and your honor. We desire only to remain here in peace."

Hosokawa said nothing as he walked off with his men into the night. For the shame of this defeat, he knew that his life would surely be demanded of him.

As the remnant of the retreating army disappeared from sight, Shirō heard the sound of his name being called from some distance. It was a deep booming voice that was intimately familiar to him. From among the first army that had appeared from the woods, emerged a man of sturdy frame and tall stature. Shirō then saw with his own eyes what his heart had already perceived. Shirō addressed the man in the only manner he had ever addressed him his entire life. "Otōsan."

十七

DEAL WITH THE DEVIL
悪魔に対処する

*"Be alert and sober of mind. Your enemy, the devil,
prowls around like a roaring lion looking
for someone to devour."*
1 Peter 5:8

*"When you talk about future plans,
the devil starts to laugh."*
Japanese proverb

"Otōsan, what would you have me do?" Iemitsu Tokugawa knelt before the ornate *butsudan* shrine in his private chamber. Spanning the length of the wall above were portraits of the deceased ancestors. He looked upon those of his father, Hidetada, and grandfather, Ieyasu. It was the latter who had won military control of the islands after the great Battle of Sekigahara, defeating his primary rival, Ishida Mitsunari, who had controlled much of the western regions.

Ieyasu had seen in the foreigners from Spain and Portugal not only the immense opportunity for trade that their ships could facilitate, but also a way of keeping the Buddhist monks in check. The Buddhist opposition to *samurai* rule,

155

coupled with their popularity among the commoners, was becoming a potential threat. The introduction of a competing religion, reasoned Ieyasu, could help offset the influence of the Buddhists.

But by the time Hidetada took power, the Christians were gaining in numbers and influence at a rate far greater than could have been predicted. Now the antidote appeared to be potentially more serious than the poison. Hidetada took measures to contain the practice of Christianity exclusively to the private realm. But this had limited effect, since the doctrines of the new religion demanded submission that was both public as well as private. And conversions continued at an alarming pace, among both noble and peasant alike.

Iemitsu gazed upon his recently deceased father's portrait. "You were wise to subdue the worshippers of the cross. But suppression is not sufficient." Iemitsu had come to regard the foreign religion as a diseased limb, one that needed to be amputated, lest the entire body become infected. What was originally presumed to be an innocuous if foolhardy cult had proven to be something subversive.

Despite being guests on the islands, the priests of this religion had the shameless audacity to publicly condemn some of the practices of their hosts. They preached, for example, that the taking of a young man into one's bed, a fairly common exercise among the warrior class, was unnatural and an abomination—"buggery" was the term they used for it. Though many of the people had come to accept the rationality of this teaching, Iemitsu was loath to allow ancient moral standards to be rewritten by those he considered *yabanjin*. Still looking up at his father, Iemitsu thought, "I will finish the task that you should have, father."

"*Tono*, the Dutchman has arrived."

Iemitsu Tokugawa did not turn to look at the servant. "Have him wait."

Captain Paul van Ricketts was chief emissary to the Japanese islands for the *Vereenigde Oostindische Compagnie.** The corporation was formed just after the turn of the century by allying several small independent trading ventures for the purpose of competing with Spain and Portugal. A British pilot who captained one of the early Dutch ships had been the first Englishman to set foot on Japanese soil. It was rumored that he had taken very quickly to the language and customs, and that he had gained the confidence of Ieyasu Tokugawa himself. It was likely only a matter of time before England joined in the rivalry for trade agreements.

But for now it was the Dutch who enjoyed the *shōgun's* favor. With them came all the trade benefits afforded by the Iberians—access to silk and spices from mainland Asia and, even more importantly, firearms from the Dutch themselves. Though the Portuguese arquebus had proven useful, the Dutch muskets and flintlock pistols were more efficient and accurate. And then there were the cannons. Much to Iemitsu's liking, the Dutch were solely interested in business. Though he cared little for their physical appearance, the "fair-haired, blue-eyed devils" were pragmatic and had no ulterior agendas. Unlike the Catholics, these men of Holland demonstrated no interest in imposing their customs. The permitting of such impositions by the Catholics had, of

---

*United East India Company, a Dutch trading company established in 1602.

course, been the grave error of the previous Tokugawas.

Van Ricketts was exceptionally tall with a slender frame that belied his physical strength. With his short-cropped straw-colored hair and beard, and large eyes of penetrating azure, he presented every characteristic Iemitsu found distasteful about the new Europeans. The Dutch captain had, up to this point, spent his time in Nagasaki dealing with the *daimyō* of the southern port regions. When he received word that Tokugawa demanded a personal audience, Van Ricketts hoped this was a sign that the overlord desired an exclusive trade agreement for the whole of the islands.

The Dutchman's own parents were among the first of the followers of Calvin to flee from France and settle in Holland. (His father had added "van" to their name as a way of assimilation.) He had for most of his young life eked out a living as a sailor and trader, contracting voyages and the sale of spices and other goods from India and the East Indies. But when the VOC became a publicly traded company and began hiring experienced seamen, Paul jumped at the opportunity. He could finally make a name for himself and bring honor to his family. The journey by sea and land from Nagasaki to Nijō Castle in Kyōto had been uneventful. He hoped his meeting with Tokugawa would be otherwise.

In the spacious common room of the castle's main keep were several guards. They kept their gazes forward, none of them making eye contact with the *gaijin*. One man, perhaps the same age as Van Ricketts, sat looking rather disinterested upon the dais. There was an unpleasant air about the fellow, and the Dutchman found himself thinking he rather hoped he wouldn't have to cross him.

A door at the rear of the room slid open and two attendants stepped through, each taking position on either side of the entry. Tokugawa then emerged. He was smaller, though every bit as regal and arresting as the Dutchman had imagined. The man called *shōgun* surveyed the room from one corner to the next, as though inspecting something newly constructed. He gave an approving nod—for what reason the Dutchman could not tell—before finally acknowledging the foreign guest.

Van Ricketts offered a sweeping, rather theatrical bow to his host. Tokugawa's expression changed abruptly to one of disdain. Little as he cared for their physical appearance, he cared even less for the flailing mannerisms of the foreigners. The exaggeration of their movements was uneconomical as well as undignified. He returned the Dutchman's gesture with a barely perceptible nod. Then he called out in a voice that was low and thunderous, "Anjin!"

Something about that word was familiar to Van Ricketts. He thought to ask a question, but knew enough to remain silent. After a few moments, another door, this one to his right, slid quietly open. From the opening emerged a man with wavy hair and a beard of silver. He had to crouch slightly in order to clear the top of the doorway. By his features, he was clearly not Japanese, though his aura and motions certainly appeared to be. He bowed simply yet reverently to Tokugawa, and then turned toward the Dutchman. He spoke in English, which Van Ricketts understood perfectly. "My name is William Adams. Lord Tokugawa has asked me to act as interpreter."

"Adams?" Van Ricketts spoke as though he were in the presence of an apparition. "The one they call Anjin? So the stories were true. You're still alive!"

"For better or for worse." The man gave a gentle laugh as the silk of his *kimono* shimmered in the natural light of the great room. "But I am not here to speak of myself. Perhaps there will be time for that later." Then, turning to Tokugawa,

"*Tono*, I am at your service." And from that point, the one called Anjin interpreted the words of Lord Tokugawa and the Dutchman to one another.

Tokugawa began, "You will be contracted to bring specified goods to and from our islands, but there will be restrictions. You will be granted permission to land in the port at Dejima in Nagasaki, but your crews will not be authorized to go outside the port area."

Van Ricketts replied, "With all due respect, Lord Tokugawa, the men must be able to move about freely after so much time at sea."

"Any provisions they require will be delivered to them—food and drink, even entertainment and women. But no foreigners will be permitted outside the port. Understand that the punishment for noncompliance will be severe."

The Dutchman looked at Adams and asked. "What does Lord Tokugawa mean by 'severe'?"

Adams replied, "Understand that in the strongest sense."

Lord Tokugawa continued, "Now, there is one other matter. In order for you to access the port, it must be secure. There is some instability in the region, and I will require your assistance in bringing the situation under control."

At this the Dutchman balked. He was well informed of the history of factions and in-fighting throughout the islands, a history that made his native Europe seem utopic by comparison. "Lord Tokugawa, please understand that I am under strict orders by my own superiors in Holland not to involve ourselves in any internal affairs."

"If you desire to conduct trade with these islands, you will abide by the conditions I set forth. The instability of which I speak was initiated by your enemies. It was the Iberians who incited the Christian converts to mount an insurrection in the port areas. This must be brought under control before the ports can be opened. I understand those in your country also worship the god-man of the cross, but do so in some other fashion and make war over it."

"Well, yes, we worship Jesus Christ, but we reject the authority of the pope in Rome and..."

"Frankly, the details of your differences are of little interest to me. My only concern, and what should be your only concern for the present, is the security of the harbor. To ensure it, I shall require a sufficient supply of firearms and ammunition. Moreover, I shall require cannons."

"Yes, well, those items can certainly be arranged," replied Van Ricketts, glad to have the discussion turned back toward business, but still uneasy about the conditions set forth.

"Congratulations, you have just made your first sale." Tokugawa turned to leave. "We will discuss the terms of payment in the morning."

With that, Adams, the Englishman who had served Tokugawa's grandfather, showed Van Ricketts to his quarters. It had been Adams, two generations earlier, who informed the first Tokugawa *shōgun* of the Iberian strategy of sending missionaries to newly discovered lands in advance of attempts to imperialize. Upon hearing of this, the elder Tokugawa immediately dismissed those Jesuit priests whom he had until then taken into his confidence as advisors. After their expulsion from the castle, Adams was the only foreigner that Tokugawa retained. And the Englishman would continue to provide counsel to both the son and grandson of Ieyasu. On this night, Adams and Van Ricketts drank together and shared tales late into the next morning.

After the *gaijin* had left the room, Tokugawa turned to Onizuka, who had remained silent and still throughout the exchange. He thought to ask Tokugawa why he had summoned the Dutchman all the way to Kyōto. Surely conditions of any agreement could have been relayed to Nagasaki. But Onizuka knew the answer. Tokugawa wanted to get a measure of the man in person, and to make very clear who would be reporting to whom.

Tokugawa spoke, "I have a task for you, young friend."

"You wish for me to take back the fortress?"

"No, I am in no haste to reclaim those ruins. We will achieve that soon enough. But before we break their bodies, I first need to break their spirits."

十八

THE RAINCOAT DANCE
蓑踊り

*"For behold, from now on all generations
will call me blessed; for He who is mighty has done
great things for me, and holy is His name."*
Luke 1:48-49

*"The goodness of the father reaches higher than a
mountain; that of the mother goes deeper than the ocean."*
Japanese proverb

After the arrival of his father, Shirō learned how word of the storming of the fortress had reached Hitoyoshi. Lord Yanazume wanted to aid in the cause of his fellow converts, but did not care to risk bringing the wrath and full force of the *shōgun* upon him. Instead, he opted to dispatch a battalion of his men, without banners and dressed in black, led by Hiromu. The plan was not without considerable risk, but it achieved the intended outcome—with the unexpected aid of the *sōhei*.

Very few of the men from Hitoyoshi had fallen during the attack, though some, including Shirō's father, had sustained injuries. Hiromu had suffered a deep gash to the shoulder.

It was not life threatening, but did require attention and rest. While he treated his father's wound, Shirō was able to convey all that had happened since the day they had last seen one another nearly two months before.

"I must say," said Hiromu to his son, "I was not pleased when I learned you had set off in search of Shinpu. He is a grown man and his fate is not your responsibility."

"I am sorry," offered Shirō. "It was perhaps foolish. I thought only of trying to save him."

"You are young and prone to acting rashly. That is not always a bad thing. I believe you did what you knew in your heart to be right, and I cannot fault you for that. I'm only grateful that you're here in the flesh. I wish I could get word to your mother."

"I find many of the claims of your religion to be quite outrageous. But even within its own dogma, there are glaring contradictions." Tomi spoke these words to Shirō as the two friends stood upon the parapet.

It had been three weeks since the soldiers from Kumamoto had been driven off. The occupants of the fortress agreed that if not for the appearance of the *sōhei* that night, the outcome would likely have been different. It turned out that the band of warrior monks had been passing through the region on their way to one of the outer islands. They had learned of the plight of the Christians and the taking of the fortress. Spying the army from Kumamoto as it marched to Yatsushiro, the *sōhei* felt a moral duty to help if they could. Shirō had invited them to remain in their company, but their leader, a man called Rennyo, said that they needed to move on. As he put it, "Though our paths were destined to cross, still they lead in different directions."

Those within the walls knew it was only a matter of time before their enemies returned in greater numbers. Each day, small parties would venture outside the fortress to forage for anything edible from the woods, or to try their luck at fishing the waters of the river. There was moderate success, though insufficient to keep up with the number of mouths to feed. There were now well over ten thousand men amongst them, not including women and children, and the supply of food was steadily dwindling.

Shirō and Tomi had spent time each day upon the parapet, keeping watchful eyes in all directions, and engaging in discourse about anything under the sun—just as they had done so often in their youth.

"What sort of contradictions?" asked Shirō.

"Well, I can think of a few," Tomi thought for a moment. "Ah, here is one! You believe that all are born with an invisible mark—an inheritance of the disobedience committed by the first man and woman, yes?"

"*Hai,*" answered Shirō. "We call that 'original sin.'"

"Yes, fine, 'original sin.'" Tomi rolled his eyes. "Some weeks before *Natāru,* you Christians celebrated a feast day concerning the mother of Iesu. You believe that she was born without the mark—this 'original sin.'"

"*Hai,*" answered Shirō. "That is true."

"Well, here's the problem. If she was of the human race, it stands to reason that she would bear this mark, if such a mark indeed exists, like everyone else. Furthermore, Christianity claims that only through baptism, instituted after Iesu entered the river, can the mark be wiped away. So, to say that Maria was born without the mark, when she obviously came before her son, is a clear contradiction."

Shirō nodded. "You certainly know more than I realized. And I thought you had no use for religion!"

"I don't," Tomi laughed. "But it's always wise to know the ways of one's enemies—even potential enemies."

Shirō joined in his friend's laughter, then took a deep breath and thought for a few moments. "Well, first of all, we believe Maria was not only born without sin—she was conceived without it in her mother's womb."

Tomi laughed again. "Ah, well, forgive my error!"

"That's quite alright," reassured Shirō, "But such details are important. As to your point, how can I explain? Because Maria was to be the mother of the incarnate God, it was necessary that she be spared from the stain of original sin, indeed of any sin. Like all of us, she too required God's grace to save her from the effects of sin. But, owing to her unique role, she was saved in a unique way."

"And I suppose you will explain that way?"

"Do you remember the day you saved me from the *inoshishi*?"

"I should hope I remember. There haven't been too many occasions on which I've saved someone from a charging wild boar!"

Shirō laughed. "I don't know all you'd been up to after you left home!" He took another deep breath of cold air. "What would you have done if the boar had wounded me?"

"Well," replied Tomi, "I suppose instead of carrying the beast back to the village as we did, I would have been forced to carry you." Tomi paused for a moment. "Although I suppose I could have just left you for the buzzards."

"Indeed, you could have done that. As it turned out, I needed you that day to save me. I was helpless, pinned against the side of that hill directly in the path of that brute."

"So, I see you've cleverly managed to change the subject. If you don't have answers to my theological questions, you could at least display some humility and admit as much. Humility is a Christian virtue, yes?"

"What I want to say is that fallen humanity is like those who have been wounded by a wild animal. They require a physician to be healed. But on that day in the forest, you saved me with your arrow before the boar's tusks could reach me. In a similar way, God saved Maria from the mark of sin before it could even touch her."

Tomi was silent for a few moments. "Hmm…An interesting answer, I'll grant you that. But if God could do that for Maria, why did he not simply do that for every…"

His sentence was interrupted by the voice of Hashizume. "Shirō, someone approaches from the south. We cannot yet tell who, but there are not so many as I might have anticipated." They looked out from the parapet onto the open field and the woods that lay beyond, the same woods from which the chanting women, followed by Shirō's father and soldiers from Hitoyoshi, had emerged a fortnight ago.

Even from the considerable distance, they could see there was something strange about the troop that approached. Many of them processed with an odd gait, as if encumbered by some weight that restrained their natural movements. They were slightly hunched over and, as they drew into closer view, Shirō and the others could see that they varied markedly in size.

As the figures approached nearer to the fortress walls, Shirō and the others realized that there were women and children amongst them. This was no army, but rather a troop of prisoners. They all appeared to be wearing an identical garment the color of dry earth that was wrapped around them like withered husks on old ears of corn.

Tomi's expression became suddenly somber. Almost in a whisper, he said, "I have seen this before."

The previous day, following the long journey from Kyōto, a battalion led by Lord Onizuka arrived at Sakamoto. Though many of the villagers had fled to the fortress, others had chosen to remain. An inspection of the homes uncovered several crucifixes, icons, and other signs of their cult. After seeing to the destruction of these, Onizuka had every soul in the village rounded up and bound. He then ordered that all the straw mats used for bedding be removed from the homes, and these were fastened to each of the peasants in the manner of a swaddling coat. The village was filled with the sound of wailing from parents and young children who were separated from one another.

Onizuka addressed them in a voice devoid of feeling, "There may be rain, even snow, on our little journey. These coats will keep you dry and protected from the elements." Indeed it did snow during the course of the three-hour trek. It was a wet and heavy snow that clung to the coats of straw. Far from protecting their wearers from the elements, the snow-laden coats became heavy and even more cumbersome to bear. By the time they arrived at the fortress, many of the children and elderly amongst them were on the verge of collapse.

Walking toward the fortress, Onizuka addressed those standing upon the parapet. "You see here some of your fellow believers. Today I bestow upon them the honor of martyrdom!" He turned to one of his men and gave a nod. The man and several others came forward with flasks. The earthen vessels were filled with rapeseed oil which they proceeded to pour onto the straw coats of the prisoners. At the same time, another one of the peasants, a village artist, was brought forward. He did not wear the coat of straw like the others. In his arms he held a canvas, a palette, and some horsehair brushes.

He was brought before Onizuka who addressed him: "You have been spared that you might serve a purpose. You will paint for posterity what you are about to witness, so that others may see the fate of those who persist in their worship of the foreign deity. Do it not, and you may join the others." Lest there be any doubt of his sincerity, Onizuka produced and held up another straw blanket. In his other hand he held a lighted torch.

Tomi drew his bow and released an arrow in Onizuka's direction, but the distance was too great. The arrow landed harmlessly and disappeared in the soft coating of snow that blanketed the otherwise barren earth. Onizuka grinned as he touched the flame to its first victim. He then went quickly down the line, igniting the straw coats until he reached the end. Their bonds ablaze, the victims began to dance around in an effort to escape the searing pain from which there was no relief. The executioners roared with laughter at the spectacle before them, while those upon the parapet could only watch in horror.

Onizuka took the hilt of his sword and pressed it hard into the shoulder of the artist. "You paint what you see now!" The artist began to wail, but Onizuka only prodded him more insistently. "Paint!" Through hot tears that streamed down his frozen face, he began to render the image of human figures engulfed in flames.

One of the children could be heard crying out, "Okāsan!" Then, a woman's voice that pierced the cold air like an arrow to the heavens, "Blessed Mother! Carry her into the arms of your Son!"

十九

Morning Miso Soup
おみおつけ

*"So teach us to number our days that we may get
a heart of wisdom."*
Psalm 90:12

*"The cherry trees put this truth very plainly:
none of the glory of the blossoms and autumn leaves
lasts long in this fleeting world."*
The Tale of Genji

For many hours, no one within the fortress walls spoke
as the smell of death clung to the air. The fragrance
of freshly fallen snow had been overwhelmed by the acrid
stench of burnt flesh, an odor so thick it could be tasted. The
smouldering bodies had been left where they lay by Onizuka
and his men, who abruptly departed from the scene after the
last one had fallen.

Amongst the charred bodies sat a lone figure. Ichiro, the
artist, his rough rendering of the scene having been pried
from his hands, was left alive. He sat motionless in the field
where the veil of snow was scarred with melted patches
surrounding the fallen bodies. On his knees with his eyes

raised to the smoke-filled sky, he held out hands stained with the colors of fire and blood. When those from the fortress went out to retrieve him, he would not stand, but nor did he resist. He merely stared into nothingness like a blind man as he was carried along with his palette and brushes back behind the walls.

As dusk approached, the *rōnin* convened to conceive a course of action. Many of the outlying villages would be in danger of meeting with the same fate as the poor souls from Sakamoto. They decided to form several companies that would depart to attempt to offer protection to those places and bring as many of the people as possible back to the shelter of the old fortress. Shirō and Tomi would lead the company headed for Takazawa. The plan was to travel south, staying off the primary road along the river as much as possible. But first they needed to bury the dead.

While they were still speaking, a solitary arrow appeared suddenly in the ground not far from where they stood in the courtyard. They stared with rapt curiosity at this protruding thing that had not been there one moment before. Tomi scrambled up to the parapet, while Hashizume cautiously ran over to the arrow and yanked it from the earth. He noticed a piece of parchment tied to the shaft. Fearing another arrow might perhaps follow, Hashizume moved hastily away from the spot.

Tomi called down from the parapet, "They've returned!" The others ran up and saw that Lord Onizuka, with his troop of soldiers, was once again standing in the field to the south of the fortress. He had apparently not gone far. To the relief of those upon the parapet, there were no other prisoners in sight. In his left hand, Onizuka clutched a long curved bow.

Hashizume removed the parchment from the arrow and unrolled it. He looked at it and then held it up for the others to see. Upon it was written: 降伏 ... *kōfuku*, the characters meaning "surrender."

"Well, I'd say that's rather unambiguous," said Tomi.

"*Hai*," agreed Shirō. "Though it would be rude not to at least offer a response."

"And I suppose you have something in mind?" replied Tomi.

Shirō climbed down from the parapet and went over to Ichiro, who was still leaning against the wall where they had set him down earlier. The blank expression on his face had not changed.

"Ichiro-san," Shirō bent down and spoke softly, "I'm wondering if perhaps I might borrow one of your brushes and a bit of paint." As soon as he asked the question, Shirō realized the unintended cruelty of this request.

Without turning his head, Ichiro simply whispered, "*Dōzo*."

Shirō took the small palette with its assortment of basic colors, and one of the horsehair brushes. He then asked Hashizume for the arrow and piece of parchment it had delivered. Sitting along the edge of the parapet, Shirō set the parchment before him with its blank side facing up. He was about to dip the brush into the small well containing red paint, still wet from Ichiro's most recent work. But just before the brush touched the paint, Shirō had another idea.

Drawing his *wakizashi* halfway out from its sheath, Shirō ran his left palm lightly along the edge of its blade. It was so sharp that he felt only a pinching sensation as the skin split. Turning his palm upwards, he dipped the brush into the small pool of blood.

Shirō rolled up the parchment and tied it back onto the arrow. Handing it to Tomi, he asked, "Would you like to do the honors?"

"Thanks, but it's your message, Tomi replied. "I think you should deliver it." He handed Shirō his bow.

Taking aim upwards, Shirō saw a big billowy cloud almost directly above them. He drew back the bow's string as far as it would stretch. A few droplets fell from his still bleeding hand. Releasing the string, he watched as the arrow flew up toward the cloud and vanished from sight.

After several moments, they saw the projectile reappear as it made its descent back to earth. It sank into the ground tauntingly close to one of Onizuka's soldiers.

"Nice shot," offered Tomi. "Although, if I had taken it, I would have at least gotten one of them in the foot."

Shirō shook his head and smiled.

The soldier stepped a few paces to the arrow and plucked it from the ground. Removing the parchment, he brought it over to his master. He unrolled it and held it up for Onizuka to see. On it was drawn, in a character that was bleeding yet still quite discernible, the single word 勝 ... *Masaru.*

The company left at daybreak, keeping along paths that were out of plain view. Shirō and Tomi walked together at the rear of the company as it made its way over the snow-blanketed terrain. They knew they would leave tracks, but they would also be able to see those of anyone who might have preceded them.

Hiromu had desired to be at Shirō's side. After their prolonged separation, his heart ached at the thought of remaining behind while his son ventured out into what had become a hostile landscape. But Shirō insisted that his father remain at the fortress. His wound was serious enough to render him of little use in a fight. Hiromu finally conceded, though not happily. As he stood with Shirō before the small gate in the wall facing the bay, he begged his son not to take any unnecessary risks. "Stay close to Tomi," he advised.

Tomi had not spoken much following the horrific scene they all had witnessed the previous day. But around midday, he finally broke his silence. "I wonder, where was your god yesterday?" Shirō did not answer, but Tomi persisted, "If your god is all loving and powerful, why did he not save those people?"

This time Shirō answered, "I believe he did."

"Did he? Then who were those poor scorched souls that we buried?"

"There is another fire—one of everlasting flames—even worse than what those poor souls had to endure. I believe it is from this fire that they have been saved."

Tomi shook his head, striding quickly ahead and out of sight.

They arrived at Takazawa village just before dusk. They had not encountered anyone the entire journey, save for an old man gathering sticks and small pieces of wood. He eyed them as they passed with a look of mixed curiosity and suspicion. He offered an obligatory bow and went about his business.

At the village, Shirō's heart sank when they discovered that no one was there. They went into every home only to find them deserted. Though there were no signs of destruction, they could only imagine the village had met with a fate similar to Sakamoto. They shuffled about in silence, looking for any clues as to what might have transpired, but there were none. One of the men approached Shirō as the outlines of the village's small buildings became harder to distinguish in the failing light. "We might as well camp here for the night. We can try our luck with one of the other villages in the morning."

"Yes," agreed Shirō. "I suppose that would be best."

Shirō and Tomi slept in the very same place they had spent the night on their previous stay in Takazawa. Father Olivera had been with them, and now Shirō wondered where his friend and mentor might be. He imagined the worst. "Tomi," he whispered. "Are you asleep?"

Tomi groaned and turned from one side to the other. "Not anymore. What is it?"

"I just had a thought. It may be a foolish hope, but I need to go and see."

The two of them walked out of the house and into the cold night air. There was just enough moonlight to navigate their way to the path that led through the woods at the village's western edge. The ground was soft underfoot save for the occasional protruding stone or twig that snapped beneath their feet. At the end of the trail, they came to the rock face of the mountain where they began to poke and prod with their weapons. Tomi remarked, "It seems no matter how many times we come here, we always go through this same ritual."

"Yes," agreed Shirō. "You'd think we could do this blindfolded by now." But after a few more minutes, they found what they were seeking. The entrance of the cave lay open before them like a hungry mouth.

They stepped in lightly for they could not see beyond the first few feet into the cavern. Tomi led the way while Shirō followed by no more than an arm's length. Tomi whispered,

"Tell me again, why are we doing this?"

Before Shirō could answer, he heard a cry followed by a dull beating sound. In the dark, he could only make out the outline of his friend's arms raised in a defensive position. Shirō's first thought was that a startled bat had attacked, but now he heard a voice that was not Tomi's.

"*Dete ike!*" The voice was forceful yet had a frail quiver. The dull blows continued to land about Tomi's upper body and arms, which he continued to hold above his head. Shirō reached out with both hands and grabbed the assailant. He was unsure of precisely what he had seized, but he thought he felt cloth in one hand and something like flesh in the other. With one powerful motion, Shirō flung the attacker out of the cave and onto the ground. He then sprang upon the prone figure and, with his hands and knees, kept it pinned to the earth. The voice squeaked, "Please, don't hurt me. I was only trying to protect myself. Please, I....."

Shirō loosened his grip. By the moonlight, he could see a face and recognized it as one of the village elders. "Ōse-san? Is that you?"

The body beneath Shirō relaxed a bit. "Who, who is that?"

"It's Shirō."

"Nakagawa-san? Oh, I am so sorry I struck you. I thought..."

"That wasn't actually me you struck. That was my friend. I'm sure he's grateful you do not have better aim!" Shirō began to laugh as he helped the old man back to his feet.

Tomi stood in the cave's entrance, rubbing his shoulder. "His aim was good enough! Ojīsan, what were you thinking? You're lucky I didn't kill you!"

Shirō asked, "Ōse-san, why are you here alone? Where are all the others?"

The old man peered out into the darkness, as though to make sure there was no one else there. Then he tugged at Shirō's sleeve and said, "Come with me!"

He led the way through the narrow passage that came to what appeared to be a dead end. Their eyes adjusted to the darkness, as cool air from above revealed that the passage continued upwards along the rock face of the wall. The old man climbed with surprising agility up a natural set of jagged steps that veered off to the right and eventually came to a landing that revealed another level of the cavern.

Shirō and Tomi were familiar with the route. They had discovered it as young boys, and it was the same way they had exited the cave on their prior visit to the village. The ceiling was low for a while, and they had to crouch to maneuver forward. Before long, the tunnel widened and they were again able to stand upright.

A soft bluish green light emanated from the end of the passage and, stepping through, they entered a large chamber with a shimmering pool of water at its center. This was the chamber in which they had taken refuge with Father Olivera following his rescue. Now, as they stood there, they saw that the space was filled with nearly a hundred of the villagers, those who had chosen to remain. And there in their midst, as though he had never left, was Father Olivera. At his feet, upon the smooth stone floor, sat Kumiko.

The men took up their arms when they saw the large crowd approaching the village. But Shirō called out, "Stand down! We are with friends!"

The astonishment over the discovery that the villagers were alive was quickly transformed to rejoicing. There was much sharing of tales into the late hours until everyone but those who kept watch slept upon their own straw mats for the first time in several nights.

The village had once again fallen quiet when Shirō and Kumiko found themselves together in a common area beside the empty *butsudan*.

"You were reckless to leave the safety of the castle," said Shirō, as though reprimanding his own child. "After what nearly happened that night in the church, you should know how much wickedness is prowling about."

"Yes, Shirō, I do know. And perhaps it was unwise for me to have ventured out on my own. But I could not sit idly knowing others were risking themselves for the sake of one another and the faith. Considering all that you have done, I should think that you would understand."

"I do understand," replied Shirō. "Still, you shouldn't have been alone."

"I had the Blessed Mother with me." Kumiko explained in detail how she had first gone to the church, what remained of it, in Hitoyoshi. She didn't know what she had hoped to find there, but something compelled her. When she arrived, she discovered that someone else was already there, sifting through the ashes as though searching for something. It was one of the old women from Takazawa. They spoke for a while, and Kumiko expressed her concern about Father Olivera. Though initially reluctant to say anything, the old woman confided in Kumiko that Shinpu was in fact safely hidden, for the time being, in the village.

Together, Kumiko and the old woman found amongst the ashes some items that were spared from the wrath of the flames—a jar of holy oil, a pouch of unconsecrated hosts, a flask of sacramental wine, and a carved wooden statue of Maria, just small enough for them to conceal in an empty rice sack.

Shirō continued to chide, "You took a great risk transporting such things here."

"*Hai*, I know that. But I also knew Shinpu would be grateful to have those items. With the hosts, he has been able to celebrate the *Misa* every day in the cave. It has become our new chapel."

Shirō felt something within him stir. He opened his mouth and words flowed out almost effortlessly. "Kumiko-san, *asa no misoshiru o tsukutte kuremasenka?*"*

---

*A traditional marriage proposal. Literally, "Would you make my morning miso soup?"

二十

JISHIN
地震

*"And they shall go into the holes of the rocks,
and into the caves of the earth, for fear of the Lord,
and for the glory of His majesty, when He ariseth
to shake terribly the earth."*
Isaiah 2:19

*"Aspire to be like Mount Fuji, with such a broad
and solid foundation that the strongest earthquake
cannot move you, and so tall that the greatest enterprises
of common men seem insignificant
from your lofty perspective."*
Miyamoto Musashi

The army marched across the field and divided into three distinct formations, each taking up position along the two land-locked sides of the fortress and the side along the river. Their number was nearly seven times that of the defeated army led by General Hosokawa the previous month. The shame of that defeat led to the order by Iemitsu Tokugawa for Hosokawa to journey to Kyōto to commit *seppuku*. Though rare for a *shōgun* himself to do so, Tokugawa

181

was pleased to be the one to remove Hosokawa's head after the general had sliced open his own belly.

Immediately following Hosokawa's execution, Tokugawa dispatched an entire brigade from Kyōto. En route to Yatsushiro, it was joined by regiments from Kobe, Okayama, Yamaguchi, Fukuoka, and, finally, Kumamoto. To the chagrin of many of the more senior officers, Tokugawa bestowed authority over the entire force to Lord Onizuka, who had already ridden ahead to the site of the uprising.

Now, as the massive force settled into position, a long train of horses and oxen came up from the rear. With great effort, they pulled something that, though set upon wheels, was large, heavy and cumbersome. Several soldiers urged the team forward as it struggled to drag the weighty thing across earth that was boggy with the recently melted snow.

While still on the road from Yatsushiro to Takazawa, Shirō had managed to catch up with Tomi when the company stopped along a tributary of the Kuma for rest and fresh water.

"I'm sorry I walked away from you back there," said Tomi. "I find much of your Christian logic vexing."

"That's alright," answered Shirō. "I quite understand. It sometimes vexes me as well."

"That cross you wear, for example. How is it that you carry and reverence a likeness of the very instrument of your beloved Savior's torture and death?"

"Because we believe that Iesu transformed that very instrument of torture and death into the instrument of redemption and life. For it is only God who can bring forth something good from something wicked."

"I see. And I suppose if the Romans had him killed in the manner of those poor villagers from Sakamoto, you might be walking around with a coat of straw rather than that cross around your neck?"

Shirō looked into the clear running water of the stream they sat beside. He picked up a small stick and drew a single straight line in the sandy soil. "When I was in Amakusa, we learned western mathematics. We studied the systems of men named Euclid and Descartes, who helped to illuminate the nature of lines and how they relate to one another."

Tomi found the names of Europe impossible to pronounce, let alone remember. "Are you changing the subject again, or is this leading somewhere?"

Shirō pointed with the stick to the line he drew. "The horizontal line, you might say, represents space. When we travel, there is a place we begin and a destination."

"Yes, Shirō, I'm familiar with the concept of lines and maps." The two laughed.

"In a similar way, the line also represents time. All events have a starting point and an ending. Our own humanity can be connected to the horizontal line, since we exist in space and time."

"Alright, Shirō, our lives are finite. We're born and we die. Dynasties and empires come and go. There may even come a day when heirs of Amaterasu are no more. I understand. What is the point you wish to make?'

Shirō poked the end of his stick into the dirt above his line. "If God is the creator and master of space and time, then he exists outside and above their boundaries. Would you agree?"

"You know I don't believe in gods, yours or any other.

But I'll grant that if someone did create time and space, something I cannot fathom and frankly which defies sense, then I suppose that someone would necessarily exist independent of those created things."

"*Hai*," agreed Shirō. "I believe this to be true. And while it may be beyond the power of our finite minds to grasp fully, it is a reasonable proposition."

"Alright, Shirō. I'll play along. Are you now going to draw a picture of your god in the dirt?"

"Well, in a sense, yes." From the point above the horizontal line, Shirō drew a vertical line that passed through it, forming a cross. "You see, it's no historical coincidence that Iesu died upon the cross. At a particular point in human history, and a particular place on earth, God entered into space and time as one of us. The cross is the union of the human and the divine. And the one who was nailed upon that intersection is both true man and true God."

A shot rang out like thunder as the earth around the fortress trembled. Before the sound was even heard by those inside, large chunks of stone from the top of the eastern wall exploded in all directions. Bodies were thrown from the parapet and slammed hard onto the ground below.

The Dutch cannon had been conveyed from the port in Yatsushiro, along with fifty cast iron balls, each the size of a man's head. Tokugawa's order had been for the army to surround the fortress, cutting off any movement in or out, thereby ensuring the eventual starvation of all those inside. But with the acquisition of the big gun, Lord Onizuka was given leave to put it to the test against the thick stone walls. Onizuka shouted the order, "Strike it again ... lower!" The adjustment was made and another iron orb loaded into the cannon. Those inside the fortress scrambled to brace the wall with timbers, even as the wounded were dragged away. Long fishing boats were also propped against the wall to offer some measure of resistance.

Another shot roared as shards of rock flew out from the center of the wall. On the inside, the percussion of the impact created a cloud of dust and small debris that dispersed and covered those in close proximity. Though the wall held fast, it was evident that each blow was exacting measurable damage.

"Again!" cried Onizuka above the din of his soldiers who were now working themselves into something of a frenzy.

Inside, bodies darted about in all directions. Most raced to distance themselves as far as possible from the assailed wall, while others continued their frantic attempts to reinforce it. Some tended the injured, while others ran about as though searching for some hidden refuge whose location had been hitherto withheld. Loud voices endeavoring to bring order to the scene drowned out the softer sound of prayers of resignation.

Then suddenly everything was still.

Birds that had been flying overhead and small animals that had been scurrying about, were now nowhere in sight. Strange blue spheres of light appeared to rise up and hover just above the earth. The clouds ceased to move as the air became motionless. Those on either side of the wall regarded one another as though some explanation might be found in the eyes of a companion.

Just as abruptly as the stillness had stifled the scene, a violent jolt shook the wall. All eyes watched transfixed as it appeared to rock to and fro. With the realization that not only the wall but the entire ground convulsed, many voices cried out, "*Jishin!*"

Outside the walls, horses reared and neighed in protest against their restraints. The men looked wildly about, instinctively seeking some route of escape. Onizuka shouted above the rumble that echoed beneath their feet. "Fools! It's a quake! Hold your formations!"

Not to be outdone by the cries of men, the earth's roar amplified, and there was an awful rending sound like a great door being pried from its frame. Soldiers spun their heads toward the sound, and stared with incredulity as whole clusters of their comrades in a moment vanished from sight.

The horses pranced about in panic as one of them sank until only its head, protruding from the grassy earth, could be seen. Soldiers scattered in all directions as a wide fissure spread, like a rent garment, in a line perpendicular to the besieged castle wall. From atop his own horse, Onizuka followed with his eyes the trajectory of the splitting earth. His eyes widened as he called out in a voice that he himself could hardly hear, "Move the cannon!"

The bronze behemoth teetered as its right wheel slipped into the crevice. The gaping mouth swallowed the fat cylinder barrel until all that was visible was the left wheel as it lay horizontal, wedged between the jagged teeth of the crevice. The canyon continued to stretch in the direction of the fortress and directly underneath the wall, finally halting halfway into the outer courtyard.

二十一

WEDDING OF THE CAVE
洞窟での結婚

*"Therefore a man shall leave his father and his mother
and hold fast to his wife, and they shall become one flesh."*
Genesis 2:24

"A woman's heart and the autumn sky."
Japanese proverb

Shirō and Kumiko knelt before the priest and the makeshift
altar behind him. Following the exchange of their vows,
Father Olivera produced a long white silken sash. It was
stitched together at the ends to form a loop, which he twisted
one time to form two nearly equal loops (what he would have
referred to in his language as a "figure of eight"). He placed
one of these loops over Shirō's head and upon his shoulders,
and likewise the other loop onto the shoulders of Kumiko.
This "yoke of marriage," as it was called, represented unity of
purpose, as with oxen bound together to pull the plough. For
the Christian, it further called to mind the promise of Iesu
when he declared, "My burden is easy and my yoke light."

The *Misa* continued with the consecration of the
elements. The pouch of hosts and a flask of sacramental

187

wine were among the items Kumiko had salvaged from the smouldering remains of the church of Saint Michael. Shirō recalled his conversation with Shinpu about how the substance of a thing could change while all outward aspects of it remained the same. Though he and Kumiko appeared little different than only hours earlier, still Shirō sensed something of his being quite altered as he felt the touch of Kumiko's shoulder pressed against his own. His mind grasped the meaning of the words the first man spoke, "This is now bone of my bones, and flesh of my flesh."

Shirō gazed upon the wooden statue of the Blessed Mother, yet another of the items Kumiko had salvaged. He noticed droplets of condensation on the surface, in the area of the face, were trickling down. It appeared as though she were crying, and a deep sorrow suddenly washed over him. It was not a sorrow that overshadowed his joy, but rather embraced it in a curious kind of dance.

"*Corpus Domini Nostri Iesu Christi custodiat animam tuam in vitam aeternam. Amen.*" Father Olivera spoke the words as he raised the consecrated host. Shirō tilted his head back slightly, closing his eyes and opening his mouth, as the priest placed the small host onto his tongue. This was Shirō's first reception of Holy Communion, and the third sacrament he received on that day.

Shirō felt a oneness not only with the woman who knelt at his side, but also with the God who created them both, the Savior who laid down his life for their salvation, and the spirit whose presence now permeated the air and stone of that cavern. As Kumiko received the Blessed Sacrament into her own body, Shirō understood they were experiencing a foretaste of heaven.

Kumiko was the first to speak after the priest had left the cavern. Glancing at the pool in its center, she said, "Well, husband, why don't you have a bath?"

Steam rose up from the water, warmed by hot rock and magma deep below the cavern floor. Shirō replied, "Tomi and I used to soak ourselves in there as kids. It is quite pleasant."

"Well, then, go ahead," she said as she began to walk away.

Shirō called to her, "Where are you going?"

Kumiko's whisper echoed in the cavern, "*Itte kimasu.*"*

Shirō paced for a bit. The enormity of all that had transpired in the weeks leading up to this day came over him in a swirling rush. When he was a boy, Shirō had travelled with his father on one occasion to Shikoku, and there saw the whirlpools of Naruto. Now his thoughts churned like those perpetually circulating waters. He tried in his mind's eye to focus on the center of those thoughts, but there was only a deep dark abyss into which he dared not stare too long for fear of falling into it.

He shook himself free of the image of the vortex and gazed upon the still water of the cavern's pool. He removed his garments, folded them neatly, and laid them upon a flat stone. Scooping up the warm water with a wooden ladle left by someone in the village, he poured it over every part of himself. Having rinsed away the dust and disquiet of the day, he stepped into the pool and reclined, resting his head against the smooth stone that contained the waters. Now he felt at ease as the liquid warmth penetrated into his muscles. He skimmed his hands lightly over the water's surface and watched the trails of blue formed by the algae.

When Shirō looked up, Kumiko was standing there at the edge of the pool. She was wrapped in a light cotton *yukata*,

*Literally, "I am going, and coming back."

a color of blue very similar to that of the cavern's glowing phosphorescence. She looked down at the floor beneath her and, untying the sash that held her robe closed, she asked, "May I share your bath?"

二十二

INOSHISHI ATTACK
イノシシの攻撃

*"And it shall come to pass in the last days, I will pour
out of my Spirit upon all flesh: and your sons and your
daughters shall prophesy, and your young men shall see
visions, and your old men shall dream dreams."*
Acts 2:17

"The caged bird dreams of clouds."
Japanese proverb

Shirō awoke with the realization that he needed to relieve
himself. He also realized that Kumiko was no longer
lying beside him. He whispered her name in the darkness,
but there was no reply. A faint light emanated from the far
end of the cavern, and so he reasoned it must be daybreak. As
he got to his feet and walked toward the light, it took on the
appearance of an illuminated portal. He stepped through it
and was startled to see people all about him. He recognized
of course the villagers of Takazawa, but also people from his
home of Watari and other surrounding places. To his left
were his parents, and on his right the family of Kumiko.
They all looked young and vibrant.

191

It occurred to Shirō that, despite having wed Kumiko in secret in order that their marriage might be sacramental, someone must have gotten word to their families. Shirō braced himself for the anticipated onslaught of either congratulations or chiding, or some combination of the two. But neither came. In fact, rather oddly, no one seemed to be paying much attention to him at all.

Shirō then realized, as though he could see from outside of himself, that he was yet a boy of only seven or eight. He further perceived that he had not stepped out of the cavern, as he initially thought, but rather into the church in Hitoyoshi. How could this be? Shirō scanned the room for Shinpu, but could not see him anywhere. Now the church was full and bustling with what appeared to be every person Shirō had ever known in his lifetime. They all looked to be in quite high spirits, as though celebrating some joyous event. Shirō's presence however went unnoticed.

After some time, the sensation of needing to relieve himself returned, so he made his way through the crowd and exited through the back of the church. He wondered how it had been rebuilt after the fire. Or had the fire been merely a dream? As he looked around for some discreet place, something large bolted from behind a nearby bush. Shirō heard a grunting followed by the rapid heavy fall of hooves upon the hard ground. He knew immediately what it was. Shirō's first thought was to run back into the church, but he feared what might happen to the others should the feral beast follow him inside. Instead, he ran out into the open, trying to escape and lead the animal away from the church.

Shirō ran with all the strength he could summon, but there was a slowness to his movements that gave him cause for alarm. He dared not look back, though he could hear the brute closing in on him. In desperation and for no rational reason he could quite grasp, he leapt into the air and began swinging his arms outward in the manner of *hira oyogi*. As he continued this motion with increased vigor, he felt his body begin to separate from the ground below. Though he could not fathom how this was possible, he found himself swimming through the air and away from the danger below and behind him.

The more powerfully he swung his arms, the more surely he floated and propelled himself through the air. If he slowed his arms to rest, he would begin to sink back toward the ground where the snorting swine continued to pursue him. But as he ascended further, the feeling of panic was overtaken by the serenity of the sky. The ceiling of clouds above him formed a pattern like billowing fish scales. In the distance, he thought he could make out a lone creature sharing the celestial space with him. As he swam gradually in its direction, he could see that it was a dove, and he had a hazy recollection of it once perching in his palm. The bird looked at him and cocked its head with a kind of casual curiosity. And then it disappeared into the clouds.

When Shirō looked down, he saw that he was now directly above Hitoyoshi Castle. The waters of the Kuma River were glistening in the sun, and the walls of the castle radiated with a whiteness that was nearly blinding. All along the river's banks, and surrounding the castle itself, was a long line of cherry blossoms in all their brilliant pink glory. It was a breathtaking sight and, for the first time since breaking away from the earth's pull, Shirō felt an exhilaration with the sensation of floating so effortlessly and being afforded this vantage of the world below. But he could see not a single soul in the castle's courtyard or anywhere else. A deep ache of loneliness overcame him, and he longed to be back in the presence of those he had left behind in the church.

With the loneliness, a feeling of fatigue began to set in. He realized he had been swinging his arms for a long time in order to remain aloft. He spied the protruding limb of a tall tree towering above one corner of the castle, and he swam his way toward it. Without too much effort, he was able to grab hold of the tree and perch himself upon the limb.

When he looked down, he saw that the boar had chased him all this way. It scratched at the earth with its front hooves, and rubbed its long curved tusks against the rough bark of the tree's trunk, as if whetting a pair of daggers. Then the beast began to strike the base of the tree with its thick skull, in an attempt to knock its prey from the limb. Fear again began to well up in Shirō. He thought to take to the air again, but doubted he could successfully do so without a running start. Then, from behind him came a voice.

"Masaru, you don't need to run."

He was startled for a moment, but the voice was familiar. After all, there was only one person who addressed him by that name. He turned and saw his Obāsan sitting quite comfortably on the limb beside his. He forgot about the danger below and smiled. "Obāsan, what are you doing here?"

"I came to thank you. Your prayers have helped me. Please continue them."

"I… I shall. Obāsan, can I stay here with you?"

She smiled. "You always had your head in the clouds. But you must go back down now. There's still much for you to do."

"*Hai,* Obāsan." Shirō looked down and saw that the boar was now patiently circling the base of the tree. "But I'm afraid that creature will devour me."

"You don't need to be afraid, Masaru. Remember what your name means. And remember too … *shisei!*" With that, she reached out and gave him a poke in the back. Then she was gone.

Shirō thought to call out to her, but he once again felt the urge to relieve himself. He decided to do so right upon the head of the beast below. He untied the drawstring of his trousers and, just as he took aim, the tree began to tremble. The entire world seemed to tremble. He slipped and wrapped his arms around the limb to stop himself from plummeting to the earth.

He reflexively closed his eyes and, when he opened them, he noticed that the wood of the limb now felt soft and supple. He could also feel that it was moving with a slight and steady rhythm. Then he perceived the sound of breathing. It was no longer the tree's limb he held in his arms. It was Kumiko.

Shirō understood he had dreamt. He also knew that he truly did need to relieve himself. He rose as gently as he could and made for the exit of the cavern. Outside, he hastily went into some bushes along the path leading back to the village. From the undergrowth came a rustling sound. Something alive was moving. The image of the boar returned to Shirō's mind, as he realized he did not have his weapon.

Then came a voice, "Hey, what's the big idea?"

Shirō jumped back. "Tomi! What are you doing here? You scared me out of my wits!"

"I scared you? I was having a pleasant dream before you decided to water my leg!"

"I'm sorry. Of course I did not know you were there. Why are you still here? Why did you not move on with the others?"

"I wasn't about to leave you two lovebirds to travel on your own. I stayed behind to give you some protection—and some male companionship. I know you're a married man now, but traveling with a woman can be a tedious affair!"

"I thank you for your thoughtfulness, old friend." The two of them began to laugh. Then Shirō added, "I am glad to see you. And I'm sure Kumiko will be nearly as surprised to see you as I was! But why on earth are you sleeping out in the cold instead of in the village?"

"I've slept in far less pleasant conditions. Anyway, the village is eerie now that it's empty. Besides, I feared you'd be on your way back to Yatsushiro before I realized you were gone."

Shirō looked up, recalling how it felt to see the world from above. "I'm not going to Yatsushiro, Tomi, at least not yet."

二十三

To Infiltrate a Fortress
要塞に潜入する

*"Behold I send you as sheep in the midst of wolves.
Be ye therefore wise as serpents and simple as doves."*
Matthew 10:16

*"You win battles with the timing in the Void born of the
timing of cunning by knowing the enemy's timing, and
thus using a timing which the enemy does not expect."*
Miyamoto Musashi, The Book of Five Rings

"What do you mean, we're not going?"

"Shinpu, see for yourself. The fortress is completely surrounded." It was the voice of Hashizume's brother, Jun, the father of the girl who had been branded in Kōnose. When the rebellion began, he was eager to help in whatever way he could, and had made his way to Takazawa. As they stood at the edge of the wood upon a low hill, Olivera saw all too clearly that the fortress was indeed encircled by troops too numerous to be counted, flying banners from Kumamoto as well as Edo and all points in between. They could also see that there was disorder below. There was much shouting, with men and horses running about in every direction. A

197

team of oxen was hitched to something that could not be clearly discerned. They attempted, albeit in vain, to hoist the thing from below the earth's surface. It was embedded in a massive crack that ran from the river bank to beneath one of the fortress walls.

"They obviously arrived here before the quake," said Hashizume's brother. On the journey from Takazawa, they too had felt the powerful shaking of the earth. But for the youngest amongst them, it was not a new experience, though every occurrence of *jishin* produced a level of fear and helplessness to which one never quite grew accustomed. "There's no way we're getting inside now. And it's perhaps just as well. Their provisions will not last much longer. The taking of the castle may have been a hasty and foolish decision."

Father Olivera marvelled at the great split in the earth. "I must get inside."

Jun snapped his head toward the priest. "Shinpu, do you not see the scene before you? There is no army on the island that is going to get past that. The best we can do now is get these poor peasants back to the village and offer them whatever protection we can. There is nothing we can do to help those inside."

"There is perhaps nothing a warrior can do, but there is much work for a priest within those walls. I must find a way."

"Shinpu, there is no way you nor any man is walking into that place."

Olivera was silent for a while as he gazed upon the river and the bay that lay just beyond. "Well," he said as he surveyed the waters, "then perhaps I shall have to swim."

On the field below, Lord Onizuka, still atop his horse, berated the men to resume proper formations. He bellowed to those fumbling with the team of oxen, "Forget the big gun! It is dead. Now leave it to its grave!"

One of the lieutenants approached him. "*Tono*, only a few more shots and that wall would be rubble!"

Onizuka ignored the remark. He pondered something as he gazed up at a wooded hill in the distance. "The quake may have hindered our progress, but it may have helped us just the same."

The lieutenant followed Onizuka's gaze toward the hill, and thought he saw a glint of something in the sunlight. "*Tono*, how do you mean?"

Onizuka did not so much acknowledge the question as continue to voice aloud the thoughts going through his mind. "The integrity of the wall has been compromised. Nature has accomplished in mere moments what would have taken weeks by the hands of men—it has formed a tunnel."

"Do you mean for us to march inside through the crevice?"

With this question, Onizuka looked sharply down, acknowledging for the first time the lieutenant's presence. "*Baka*! Are you volunteering to be the first to march through the crevice? We will not break a dam with a mere trickle. We will cram the crevice beneath the wall with Dutch gunpowder and send it tumbling down. Then we rush in like a *tsunami* upon the renegades."

Well into the darkness of night, a small light appeared at the confluence of the Kuma and Mae rivers. The light floated gently along the Mae which veered slightly to the north, while the wider Kuma continued its straight run west to the bay. Both emptied into the harbor on opposite ends of a small island just west of the fortress grounds. The light might have gone unnoticed on most occasions, but in the camp there were watchful eyes in all directions. Lord Onizuka indeed took notice of the gradually growing flicker that reflected on the water's shimmering surface.

"What is that boat doing out here at this hour?" His question, though not directed toward anyone in particular, demanded an answer.

"*Tono*," responded one of the men, "It is an *ushō*."

"*Ushō?*"

"*Hai, Tono.* One of the cormorant fishermen. They have a royal license to fish these waters at night."

"I see. Well, it's good to know royal authority is still being exercised in practical ways." There was a low rumble of laughter that diminished almost as quickly as it erupted.

One of the men spoke up. "*Tono*, will we bring down the wall tomorrow?"

Onizuka appeared momentarily offended, as though someone had insulted his mother. "Tomorrow? No, these traitors won't get away so lightly. They must be made to suffer. I want them feeble with fear and hunger before we bring down the wall."

He paused for a few moments. "How many *inoshishi* were killed in today's hunt?"

"About thirty head," someone answered, "perhaps forty."

"Good. Prepare pits for roasting. I want the rebels to be awakened by the smell of succulent meat in the morning."

"*Hai, Tono!*" The man turned away to carry out the uncomplicated order.

Onizuka called out to him, "Save and collect the fat from the beasts. We shall have some use for it."

The fisherman took a length of cord and tied it loosely around the long slender neck of the bird wedged between his knees. As was the custom, a team of twelve cormorants accompanied him on each nightly hunt. Those standing along the shore observed with genuine curiosity the ancient ritual, passed down for generations from fathers to sons. With their nooses fashioned and fitted, the birds, tethered by much longer cords to the hand of the fisherman, were released into the water. Within minutes the birds began returning to the boat, their raptor mouths filled with large fish that their throat cords prevented them from swallowing. The fisherman deftly coaxed the fish from the gullets of the birds. After loosening their restraints, he rewarded them with smaller fish, kept stored in a wooden barrel at the boat's stern. The fisherman picked up his oar, paddled farther downstream for some distance, and repeated the process.

From the bottom of the boat came a low voice. "Are we out of sight from the shore?"

"Nearly, Shinpu. I'm taking my time and following my usual routine."

"I know you risk much in doing this."

"Not at all, Shinpu. I suspect their main concern is that no one brings food to the fortress."

"If you get me as close to the rear wall as possible, I will swim to the shore."

"These waters are icy cold. This will all be for naught if you freeze to death."

"I'll be alright. My bigger concern is getting inside once I'm ashore."

The river made a slight bend to the south, and before long the lights and silhouettes on the shore disappeared from sight. The fisherman rowed toward the shore of the castle's rear wall, getting as close as he could without running aground upon the large rocks beneath.

"This is as close as I can get, Shinpu."

Though he could clearly make out the stone outline of the wall, Olivera knew it would still be a swim of some distance. But there was no turning back. Stiff from lying so long against the boat's hard bottom, still he managed to pull himself up and slip into the frigid water. He gasped and summoned the will to propel himself forward.

二十四

REUNIONS
再会

*"You have given a banner to those who fear you,
that it may be displayed because of the truth."*
Psalm 60:4

*"Today is victory over yourself of yesterday; tomorrow is
your victory over lesser men."*
Miyamoto Musashi

"Almost there."

Kumiko was the first to spy the bright red *torī* gate of Aso-jinja, the Shintō shrine just across the river from the grounds of Hitoyoshi Castle. The journey from Takazawa had taken only a few hours, and the chill of the early morning air had given way to the kind warmth of the late March sun. As the three walked along the path that followed the Kuma River, Kumiko pointed out the names of the flowers that were beginning to bloom. She knew them all. There were the brilliant yellows of the buttercups and amur adonis, the white pot-shaped andromedas, and the pale pink blossoms of the star magnolia trees. Kumiko's favorite was the deep rose-colored camellia, with its bright yellow stamen in the center. She bent down to pick one and placed it in her hair, just above her left ear.

The town was relatively quiet when they arrived. A few merchants transported their wares across a bridge, while groups of small children played in the streets. Passersby stared at the three of them, mainly on account of Shirō's attire. On the way to Hitoyoshi, they had first stopped at Shirō's home in Watari. The house was empty, and Shirō made the hopeful assumption that his mother was still at the castle. Looking through the house for anything that might prove useful, Shirō noticed the Portuguese costume Father Olivera had presented him for his sixteenth birthday. Shirō never had occasion to wear it, but desiring a change of clothes, he decided to put it on.

Tomi took one look and laughed. "Are you going to wear that in public?"

But Kumiko added, "I think it looks quite regal!"

The reaction of the guards at the castle gate was one of curiosity. One of them, after giving Shirō's garb a cursory examination, asked without expression, "What is your business here?" Shirō thought of any number of responses he could have given, but he answered simply, "I wish to see my mother."

A woman standing upon the parapet saw the figure approach and her heart leapt. She had been looking out across the expanse of the bay and, by the pale light of the stars, she could see the rhythmic rise and fall of the waves. The sound of the water lapping against the shore was soothing, and carried with it echoes of happier times. Something in the distance caught her eye. It was the solid shape of something. A boat? Yes, it was a boat. Transfixed, she gazed at the small wooden vessel as it bobbed and rolled with the motion of the current.

Her attention was arrested by another movement, this one on the shore. It was a human figure. It teetered as it made its way toward the western wall of the fortress. She was about to cry out a warning, but there was something familiar about the approaching form. She strained to see better and, as the man—for she could now clearly see it was a man—neared the wall, he began to falter. Then she recognized him. She called down from the parapet, "It's Shinpu!" Several others ran over and looked down to see the wet figure of a man stumbling across the stones. In his arms there appeared to be something clutched tightly to his chest. Three of the men ran out quickly from the narrow *uzumimon* gate. Just as they reached him, he collapsed on the rocky beach.

Shirō found his mother lying atop a *futon* arranged in the far corner of the room. Her belly was far rounder than it had been the day Shinpu was first taken away. That day now seemed a lifetime ago. He walked over and knelt down at her side. Being in the presence of his mother brought Shirō great joy, but he was also acutely aware of how much he missed his father. His parents had always complemented one another in such a way that the absence of one seemed to diminish the other. Still, the sight of his mother, and the unborn child within her, made the spirit of his father felt.

Michiko took her son's hand into hers and placed it against her abdomen. Shirō felt something strike firmly against his palm. His eyes widened and he looked from their hands to his mother's eyes. She smiled.

"Does it hurt?" he asked. Shirō's studies in Amakusa had not yet extended to the realm of *sanka*.

"No," she replied, still smiling. "Your kicks were even stronger!"

"Okāsan, much has happened since we were last together." Shirō stood and brought the young woman beside him forward. "I have taken Kumiko as my wife."

Michiko closed her eyes. Shirō could not tell whether this was a sign of her displeasure, or perhaps a reaction to another one of the baby's sudden movements. But as she opened her eyes, there was a glow about her.

"She is a good woman," said Michiko, now smiling at Kumiko. "And comes from a good family. One of the *nakōdo* could not have made a better arrangement."

Shirō stepped to one side to allow his mother to see Tomi, who had been fidgeting in a corner near the doorway. "Okāsan, you remember Tomi, don't you?"

"Oh my, Tomi-kun, it's been quite a long time. You're so grown up now!"

Tomi bowed and, for a moment, Shirō feared his mother might bring up the incident with the *suika*, though he knew she would never do such a thing. Instead she said, "I see you are wearing the Portuguese apparel from Shinpu."

"*Hai*. I retrieved it from the house before coming here."

"Your father and I thought perhaps you might wear it on the day that was to be your first communion, but you were reluctant."

"I admit, I did not want to stand out. As the saying goes,

*Deru kugi wa utareru.** But now that I wear it, I rather like the way it feels."

The trousers were of a *pantalonas* style cinched just below the knees. Their color was a deep azure, and there was a matching vest with a large golden cross embroidered upon the chest. Beneath the vest was a scarlet shirt, thick in the manner of *tanzen*, with billowing sleeves. Around the waist was tied a long sash of white linen which secured his swords. The one article he omitted was the ruffle collar, partly because it was too frilly, but mostly because it inhibited the free movement of his head. Also, he did not wear the European boots, which he found too stiff. Instead he wore split-toe long *tabi* socks and sandals.

Kumiko spoke. "Nakagawa-san, when will the baby arrive?"

"If he had his way, he'd be out already!"

"You believe it's a boy?"

"*Hai.*"

A guard entered the room and bowed. "Master Nakagawa, Lord Yanazume has requested your presence."

When he opened his eyes, he did not immediately know where he was. He felt something rigid supporting the small of his neck and a thick blanket covering his body. He looked about the room which was bare, but for a wooden carved crucifix on a wall to his right. Trying to raise himself up, he felt dizzy and weak. He allowed his head to sink back down

---

*The stake that sticks up gets hammered down.

as he let out a soft groan. A *shōji* at the far end of the room slid open, and a middle-aged woman appeared. She greeted him softly yet cheerfully, "*Ohayō gozaimasu*, Shinpu-sama."

Olivera reflexively replied in kind, startled by the raspiness of his own voice. "Am I in the castle?" he managed to croak.

"*Hai.* You were brought in, but not before you collapsed on the beach. You are safe now, and I'm sure you are famished." She placed before him a bowl of cloudy broth. "*Sumimasen,*" she said as she lowered her head, "I wish there were more to offer."

He managed to sit up, and drank the broth. It was hot, but he drank it quickly. The *shōji* once again slid open. This time a familiar face, that of Hashizume, appeared in the doorway.

"Shinpu!" he exclaimed. "We thought perhaps we'd gotten you inside only to lose you! It is good to see you among the living."

"Yes," replied Olivera, "It is good to be among the living."

"My heart is glad to see you, but I must ask why on heaven and earth did you risk getting here? Did you somehow not notice the multitude surrounding the place? You are quite fortunate not to be roasting out there along with the *inoshishi* upon which they are feasting. What were you thinking to come here?"

"I know it may appear foolhardy, but I believe you may have need of a priest here."

Hashizume let out a small laugh and nodded. "We have need of any man we can get, but yes, of a priest especially so." Then he produced a leather pouch which Olivera immediately recognized. "We found this tucked into your sash. We were not going to take the liberty of opening it unless, well…"

This time the priest let out a small laugh. He felt his strength slowly starting to return. "Unless I died? Go ahead and open it."

Hashizume took the pouch, which was still damp, and opened it. Inside there was a thick cloth that had been folded several times. Setting the pouch aside, he placed the cloth onto the floor and began to unfold it. Many people, upon hearing that the priest had awakened, had come into the room. Hashizume continued to unfurl the fabric before him. Fully opened, it occupied a sizable area of the floor. There were small gasps as the people looked upon the unfurled banner.

It was made of tammet, a lightweight worsted wool fabric. Along the top were seven stitched loops, large enough to accommodate a thick rod for hanging. Seven more such loops ran down its right side. It was an earthen color, faded in many places from time and the elements. In the center was the image of a bronze chalice, directly above which was a consecrated host bearing the image of a cross. On either side of the chalice was an angel, adorned in colors of red and blue, and kneeling in adoration of the Blessed Sacrament. At the top of the banner was the Portuguese inscription, *"Louvado Seja o Santíssimo Sacramento."**

That night, some of the women found a long pole and, at dawn, the banner was raised high atop the parapet of the central wall for their enemies to plainly see.

Somewhere out beyond the waters of the bay, just off the coast of Amakusa to the west, another ensign was hoisted high and fluttering in the wind. It bore the orange, white, and blue horizontal stripes of the Dutch flag, flying upon the mast of the *Griffioen* as she slowly made her way eastward.

---

*Praised be the most Holy Sacrament.

二十五

ONWARD CHRISTIAN SAMURAI
キリスト侍の出陣

*"Let us not grow tired of doing good, for in due time we
shall reap our harvest, if we do not give up."*
Galatians 6:9

"Fall down seven times, get up eight."
Japanese proverb

Shirō entered the room and saw a large gathering of men.
In the previous weeks, Lord Yanazume had summoned
Christian *daimyō* and *samurai* from around the region. They
came from Ebino and Uemura to the south, from Minamata
and Izumi to the west, from Nishiki and Yunomae to the
east, from Itsuki and Kuma to the north, and many points in
between. Shirō bowed to Yanazume, who motioned for him
to take a seat upon an unoccupied *zabuton*.

Yanazume addressed the room, "I have invited young
Nakagawa to join us. He has come from Yatsushiro where
his father still holds control of the fortress with a number
of our people exceeding *ni-man*—quite possibly more. The
grounds are now surrounded by a force three times that

number. There is no way in or out, and all lines of supply and communication have been cut off. From our best estimation, there is likely little food remaining. Even without launching a full-out assault, the enemy will very soon have starved all within those walls."

He paused for a moment before continuing.

"There is more. As some of you know, we attempted to dispatch supplies there several days ago. We hoped a smaller boat might go undetected by approaching the rear of the fortress from the bay side. The plan might have been successful, but there was a Dutch ship with the big guns anchored in the bay. According to a scout, the ship of the blue eyes blew our supply vessel out of the water without warning or provocation. It is now clear that Tokugawa has contracted the aid of the new foreigners against us."

This revelation was followed by a prolonged murmur throughout the room.

What Yanazume nor anyone else in the room could know, because there were no survivors to tell the tale, was what those on the supply boat had seen just before making contact with the Dutch ship. As they made their approach from Iwa Island to the west, they spied upon the shore just at the headwaters of the Mae River, the outline of a solitary crucifix on the beach. They initially took this as a sign of hope. But hope quickly turned to horror as they saw a man hanging upon the cross. From his rib cage protruded the shaft of a spear. A group of cormorants, their tethers tied to the foot of the cross, pecked at the feet and legs of their former master.

Yanazume called the room to order. "The question I have summoned you to decide is this: what course of action do we now take?"

There was a long pause. One of the elders, Lord Kuga of Uemura, was the first to speak. "It is clear to me that there is really nothing to discuss. We are vastly outnumbered. And now, considering the aid of the Dutch, there is little we can do. Those who took the fortress acted rashly. They made their decision and sealed their fate just as surely as they sealed themselves within those walls."

To this, Lord Tomojiri of Nishiki replied, "I would not be so quick to judge the commoners as having acted rashly. While we had rice in our bowls every evening, they did not. And they've endured increasing abuse for the sake of The Way. Whether taking the castle was logistically prudent, that debate is of no use now. The question is, do we merely sit idle while our brethren in Christ starve to death?"

The next to speak was Lord Ikeshita of Kuma. "I believe no one here is addressing the larger issue. The demise of those in the old fortress is, I fear, a sad but foregone conclusion. I agree with Lord Kuga that there is nothing we can do for those inside. But what of our own fate? Tokugawa has exceeded his father's disdain for The Way to a degree we could not have predicted. Like the faithful of ancient Rome, it may be time for us to put our heads down, lest we find them severed from our bodies."

With these words, a great commotion erupted in the room. Some shared nods of agreement with those seated beside them, while others wagged fingers and shouted across the room. A few remained seated and silent, with expressions that conveyed a sort of sad surrender. This continued for a while until, finally, Lord Yanuzume struck his fist hard upon the book of poetry on the table before him.

Every head snapped toward his direction and the room fell silent. Yanazume cleared his throat and spoke, "It is plain that we have at least two opposing camps in this matter. I understand that all here have much to lose. If we openly march against Tokugawa, the odds are not in our favor. If we do nothing, many will die, though our own skins might be spared ... perhaps, for now. I have thus far not heard any other options given voice. Are there, I wonder, any worthy of consideration?"

There was some dull grunting and shaking of heads. Before it could escalate into anything greater, Yanazume cut through it with a question. "What say you, Master Nakagawa? I wish to hear your thoughts."

Shirō had been silent but attentive the entire time. His mind had also raced with colliding thoughts and images from the past days and weeks—thoughts of his parents, Tomi, Shinpu, and Kumiko. There were also flashes from his dreams—of swimming in the air, the boar, and the dove. Then there were those things, like the cave and the weeping statue of the Blessed Mother, that seemed to float between the realms of dream and reality.

But even with all these thoughts echoing off the walls of his mind, there was a calm and a stillness in his heart. He felt the presence of someone with him. It was a nameless yet familiar presence. Though not visible, the presence was more real to him than that of any man in the room. The presence rose up and Shirō rose with it.

The small band of men rose up from the long shadow of the wall and rushed out into the night.

The food supply in the fortress had dwindled to nearly nothing. Whatever scant scraps remained were rationed to the children and elderly. The others had resorted over the past few weeks to eating grass and other wild vegetation, even whatever insects or earthworms that could be dug up from the ground, which was just beginning to show signs of spring thaw.

It was Yoshimura who proposed the plan of staging a raid on the enemy camp. Perhaps it was the smell of roasting meat wafting over the walls that produced the final straw. The others had dismissed any attempt to venture outside the walls as nothing more than a suicide mission. But none could argue that their days were becoming markedly numbered.

The plan, if it could even be called such, was for a party of perhaps fifty to run out under cover of darkness. They had observed that, after the great roasting of *inoshishi*, many large sacks were filled and brought to one particular tent that stood apart from the others in the camp. At night, no one was observed retiring to this tent. Those inside the fortress surmised that the sacks contained foodstuffs, perhaps even the remains from the boars. Why these would be stored in sacks, they could not be certain, but if true, anything from which to produce a broth would go a long way to feed many.

They would steal into the tent, grab whatever they could lay hands upon, and somehow manage to get back to the fortress. They knew nothing short of a miracle would be required, and they fervently prayed for precisely that.

This night the moon was but a sliver, and the cover of clouds thick. Upon the parapet, archers waited at the ready to give cover to their comrades on the ground, though the odds of striking one of them were just as good as hitting one of the enemy. Among those volunteers in the party were Hashizume, Yoshimura, and Kuritani. Father Olivera had also asked to join, but none of them would hear of it. His ministry to those within the fortress would be needed until whatever end they might meet.

The party exited through the bayside *uzumimon* gate, the same one they'd used to retrieve Father Olivera nearly a month earlier. It was most unfortunate that there were enemy soldiers who had spied the priest stumbling onto the shore. Though they could not reach him before he was pulled into the fortress, they did deal with the fisherman who aided him in getting there.

Crawling on their bellies along the base of the wall, they made their way to the edge of a sparse wood at the northern end of the fortress. Once behind the cover of trees, they still kept low as they made their way in slow silence around the perimeter of the enemy's camp. After nearly an hour, they came to the place where the supply tent was pitched, a distance of about one *chō* from the edge of the wood. Incredibly, there appeared to be no one inside, nor even anyone guarding it. There was, however, the sight of many torches at some distance, and sounds of the soldiers entertaining themselves.

Hashizume knew that hesitation would be their greatest enemy. With a wave of his hand, he signalled the others to get into the tent. Crawling beneath its rear flap, one by one they entered. From corner to corner, there were sacks piled ten to twelve high. Taking a long knife from his obi, Hashizume thrust it into one of the sacks. He slid it back out and smelled it. "Definitely meat," he whispered. "Everyone, grab a sack and get out of here, *hayaku!*"

They filed out from a slit in one of the side flaps, each man with a sack over his shoulder, and headed back in the direction of the wood. As they rounded the corner of the tent, they immediately saw a bright light. There were two soldiers, less than a stone's throw from the tent. One was squatting down to relieve himself. The other, who held a lit torch, looked directly at the intruders. Before he could make a sound, Hashizume pounced. Allowing his sack to drop, he lunged forward and clamped a hand over the standing man's mouth. With his other hand, he plunged his knife, still greasy with meat, into the man's sternum. In the same moment, Kuritani drew his *katana*, and lopped off the head of the squatting man before he'd even finished answering nature's call.

Retrieving their sacks, Hashizume and Kuritani motioned for the others to make haste to the cover of the wood. Yoshimura spied the still lit torch upon the ground, and an idea entered his mind. He grabbed the torch and held it to the loose folds of the tent, hoping to create a diversion. The structure did indeed go up in flames very quickly. But what Yoshimura did not anticipate was that the fire would illuminate the entire area, exposing them all.

Hashizume looked at Yoshimura, still holding the torch, and yelled, "You fool!" The look of remorse on Yoshimura's face lasted only a moment before an arrow lodged itself into the side of his neck. A flurry of arrows followed, many of them finding human targets. Hashizume winced as one sank deep into his thigh. Those still standing turned to run, but the enemy was soon upon them in overwhelming numbers. The sounds of clashing steel were short lived as every member of the party was cut down, not one of them making it to the wood. Hashizume was the last to fall, but not before taking down as many as seven of the enemy with him.

Lord Onizuka arrived and surveyed the scene. He would demand an explanation later as to how the camp perimeter could have been breached. For the time being, he was more interested in the rebel bodies lying before him. He ordered one of the soldiers, "Cut them open!"

The young soldier appeared confused. "Excuse me, my lord?"

"I said, cut them open! I want to see what they've been eating!"

The soldier just stood there looking bewildered. Onizuka grabbed hold of the soldier's sword and pushed him aside. He drove the sword into the belly of Yoshimura and sliced downward. The intestines spilled out, followed by a pungent odor. The young soldier, his eyes wide, turned and vomited. Onizuka gave a smirk and poked with the tip of the sword through the gelatinous pile until he found what he was looking for—bits of decayed leaves and what appeared to be pieces of cloth, like that of a rice sack.

"As I suspected," muttered Onizuka to himself. "They've run out of food entirely." He turned to face the men, "Gather up those sacks and put out that fire! Tomorrow, we end this."

二十六

WALLS FALL
外壁が落ちる

*"If either of them falls down, one can help
the other up. But pity anyone who falls
and has no one to help him up."*
Ecclesiastes 4:10

*"A friend is one who knows you,
and loves you just the same."*
Japanese proverb

"That was quite some speech you gave in there." There
was genuine admiration just beneath Tomi's tone of
benevolent mocking. "I didn't know you had it in you!"

"Yes, well," replied Shirō, "neither did I. How did you
hear? Were you eavesdropping?"

"Of course I was. And I think the lot of you are insane."

"You may be right, Tomi, but I prefer this breed of
insanity over despair and surrender."

"Well, if you are insane, then I suppose I'm a complete
lunatic for going along with you."

Shirō replied, "No, Tomi. This is not your fight. You have
nothing at stake here. You have your whole life and many

219

adventures yet ahead of you."

They had been walking together, but now Tomi stopped in his tracks. He had an expression as though he'd been slapped in the face. "How can you say that to me after all we've been through? Look, I don't believe all that you believe. I don't believe in virgin births, or men who can walk on water and come back from the dead. I don't believe in bread becoming flesh, or invisible powers. I don't believe in heaven or hell. I trust my own senses, and I believe in what I can see and touch."

Shirō smiled. "And our friendship, Tomi-san? Can that too be reduced only to what you can see and touch?"

Tomi threw his head back and laughed. "You see, Shirō, that's just the sort of question that keeps me in your friendship! I don't believe all you believe, but the things you believe do make for stimulating discussion. And that's one of the reasons I must go with you. You'll have a much better chance of coming back alive if I have your back. And I want to keep you alive so we can continue these discussions a while longer!"

Now it was Shirō's turn to laugh. "So, I see! It's for entirely selfish reasons you wish to help ensure my well being!"

"Well, mostly, I suppose. But if you require a nobler reason, I have one for you. Though I don't share your theology, nor even much of your philosophy, I do recognize a bully when I see one. And you know how I feel about bullies."

"Well, old friend, it sounds as though you've made up your mind." Shirō paused and looked into Tomi's eyes, as if probing for something.

"What is it?" asked Tomi.

"I was just thinking that you would make a formidable Christian."

"*Haite mo ii desu ka?*"* Kumiko stood at the guest room's open doorway.

The response came instantly, almost reflexively. "*Hai dōzo.*"†

"*Ojama shimasu!*"‡ Kumiko slipped softly into the room, her feet covered by her full-length *yukata*. "Nakagawa-san, I hope I am not disturbing you."

"*Iie, iie.* I have had more than enough rest these past weeks. I am glad you have come. After all, you are now my daughter-in-law."

"*Hai,*" replied Kumiko softly. "I, I am sorry that perhaps we acted rashly. We both wanted the blessings of our families, but..."

Michiko smiled. "You have no need to apologize. The truth is I had always hoped something might grow between you and Shirō. You have been friends since childhood, and friendship is the best foundation on which to build a strong marriage. You have my blessings, though you may have gotten more than you bargained for with me for a mother-in-law!"

Kumiko smiled and bowed gently. "I am honored to have you for a mother-in-law. And I feel especially blessed to soon be having a sister-in-law."

Michiko placed her hands over her belly. "Oh, you think it is a girl?"

---

*"Is it alright to enter?"

† "Yes, by all means."

‡ Literally, "I am committing the rude act of intruding." A polite expression to use when entering someone's space.

Kumiko's face reddened slightly. "Oh, I do not know why I said that. I suppose I've always wished for a little sister."

Michiko waved her hand to brush away Kumiko's embarrassment. "I really don't know which it is. I told Shirō I think it's a boy because I know he's always wanted a little brother."

Kumiko's shoulders sank a bit. "You know they leave in the morning for Yatsushiro."

"*Hai*," replied Michiko, "I know."

"Everything in my heart cries out to stop him from going. And yet, I cannot ask him to be anything other than what he is."

"That is one dilemma of the human heart—having to let go of those we love, knowing that it may bring pain to them and, consequently, to ourselves."

"Okāsan," Kumiko addressed her mother-in-law as such for the first time. Taking a beaded cord from the sash of her *yukata*, she asked, "Will you pray with me?"

"*Hai*, musume-san," answered Michiko. "Let us pray."

Lord Onizuka stood upon the field and scanned the length of the eastern-facing fortress wall. The sun was just coming up behind him as one of the soldiers approached. "*Tono*, we have recovered all the sacks of the animal fat."

Onizuka answered without looking at the man. "Pack them tightly into the crevice beneath the wall."

"*Hai, Tono!*" The soldier could only guess at the purpose of this order. He knew better than to ask directly.

Just as he left to carry out the order, another soldier

approached. "Onizuka-sama, a rider from Kuma has arrived. He says he seeks an audience with you. He claims to have information."

"Information? What sort of information?" His excellency, Jorge Maldonado, bishop of Macau, sat in his office dealing with the temporal matters of the day over tea, when his secretary entered with a small man who appeared to be one of the natives.

"Your Grace, forgive the intrusion. But this man claims to be a courier from the Empress Meishō herself. He bears a letter that she strictly ordered be placed into no one's hands but yours, directly."

"The empress?" replied the bishop, setting down his cup. "This is certainly most out of the ordinary. Do you believe he is in earnest?"

"The letter does seem to bear the official seal, Your Grace. I am familiar with it from my time there."

"Well, then, let's have a look." The bishop reached out his hand. The courier passed it to him ceremoniously with both hands and a low bow. The man appeared weary, but the bishop did not offer for him to sit.

The bishop carefully opened the envelope and removed a thick sheet of folder paper. "I suppose you will need to translate this for me, Martim," he said to his secretary. "My Japanese is quite limited." He unfolded the letter and examined the writing. "Oh, it's composed in Latin. Yet another surprise." He sat down and put on a pair of spectacles as he began to read.

Onizuka regarded the man coolly, looking up only for a moment as he meticulously ran his blade to and fro against a whetting stone. Looking back down to his work, he said, "I know you, yes?"

"*Hai, Tono!* We met in Edo in the spring of last year."

"Yes, I never forget a face. Ikeshita, no?"

"*Hai*, of Kuma Village. I'm flattered that you remember."

"And why have you come to Yatsushiro alone? Why have you not brought your own personal guard at least to aid in the recapture of this fortress? If all the *daimyō* of this region were loyal, I should have had little need to make the long journey from Kyōto. Yet, alas, here I am."

"*Sumimasen*, Onizuka-sama. I wanted to come as swiftly as possible. I come with something more valuable than men. I have information."

"Yes, so I've heard." Onizuka paused and set his sword beside the whetting stone. "Go on."

"As we speak, a sizable force is assembled and preparing to depart from Hitoyoshi Castle. They mean to engage you and bring supplies to the rebels. They are led by a young Christian by the name of Nakagawa. Many believe he is some kind of messiah whose triumph was prophesied. They will be here within two or three days."

Onizuka smiled. "By that time, there will be nothing for them to see but the headless corpses of their fellow believers. But we will see to it that they do not arrive. And you will help to make it so."

Ikeshita began to fidget. "What would you have me do?"

"I'll give you specific instructions. Just be sure you carry them out, or you may share the same fate as the fools inside those walls."

"*Hai, Tono.*" Ikeshita was already beginning to regret his betrayal.

The signal was given from shore and a plume of smoke could be seen rising from the bow of the *Griffioen*. Moments later came a boom like thunder that shook the air and echoed back from the forest in the distance. Stone scattered in all directions from the seaward-facing wall of the fortress. Those inside scurried away from the force that percussed through the wall, into the ground, and up into their very bones. Dust and large bits of debris hailed down all about them.

The ship made its way from the bay to the mouth of the river. Another shot was fired, this one landing inside the grounds. This time, bodies were hurled and broken like weightless sticks through the air. The people, disoriented with hunger and fatigue, ran about aimlessly, perhaps with the hope that the mere act of movement might prolong life. The *rōnin*, for their part, did what they might to get the others to take cover. Many of the children and elderly crouched down in the central courtyard, as Father Olivera performed the rite of general absolution, though what sins these poor souls might have, he could not imagine.

For many long minutes, the cannon blasts were incessant, each one claiming a portion of wall and human nerves. Hiromu Nakagawa could see the mast of the Dutch ship glide slowly over the top of the castle wall facing the river.

He scrambled up to the parapet, expecting the wall to crumble from beneath him at any moment. He could see a man standing, waving his arms, on a platform near the top of the mast. Though Hiromu could not understand the shouts coming from the man, nor the responses from the crew below, he could tell that the Dutchman was directing them where to aim the big guns. For one brief moment, Hiromu looked directly into the foreigner's steely blue eyes.

Hiromu raised his bow, took aim, and loosed an arrow. It sank deep into the wood of the barrel-like structure in which the blue-eyed man stood. The Dutchman swung his leg over the side of his perch to descend out of harm's way. That was a fatal mistake. Hiromu had already nocked another arrow. He let it fly and it found its mark directly in the soft tissue at the back of the foreigner's skull. It went through, sending the shaft jutting from the man's mouth. He fell in a heap and his ankles became ensnared in a web of rope. The body dangled and spun around, looking like some macabre wind vane.

But the cannon fire did not cease. The men on the ship took aim with their flintlock rifles and sent up a volley at the spot where Hiromu stood. He dove down behind the parapet, but not before a searing pain ripped through his left shoulder. As the sailors took time to reload, Hiromu summoned the strength to get back to his feet and let another arrow fly. He could not hold the bow steady, and the arrow embedded itself harmlessly in the ship's deck.

In the next instant, another arrow appeared beside Hiromu's errant flight. He turned to his right to see he'd been joined by several of his companions. They proceeded to send down volleys onto the ship's deck, keeping the sailors there pinned down. What none of the men on the parapet perceived was the mouth of a big gun aimed directly at them. There was a flash, followed by smoke, and then nothing but a gaping hole where Shirō's father and his companions had stood.

Outside the eastern wall of the fortress, Lord Onizuka shouted the order, "Light the powder!" A long line of gunpowder ran along the ground and beneath the fortress wall, into the crevice the earthquake had created some eight weeks before. A soldier wielding a torch came forward and lowered it to the earth. The powder ignited, and all eyes were fixed as the bulb of fire steadily made its way along the ground toward the castle.

二十七

GOOD FRIDAY
聖なる金曜日

*"Greater love hath no man than this, that a man lay
down his life for his friends."*
John 15:13

*"This is the truth: when you sacrifice your life, you must
make fullest use of your weaponry. It is wrong not to do
so, and wrong to die with a weapon yet undrawn."*
Miyamoto Musashi

In the morning, Kumiko helped her husband to dress.

"Please come back to me," she said as she tied the silk
sash around his waist. "I should very much like to raise a
family, you know."

"*Hai*," answered Shirō, as he poked her playfully just
beneath her navel.

"Don't worry, Kumiko-san." It was the voice of Tomi
standing in the doorway. "I'll keep a close eye on him."

Shirō had already said farewell to his mother. She was
stoic, though he knew she was beside herself with sorrow.
She feared she had lost him once. He had returned only to
depart again into graver danger than before.

229

Shirō was summoned to the inner courtyard, where he found Lord Yanazume standing beside a beautiful white horse. "This is Takeo," said Yanazume. *Takeo* was an ancient word for warrior, or more precisely, for military virility. "He is the best of my stable."

"He is a magnificent creature," said Shirō, admiring the animal's powerful form and the brilliant sheen of its coat.

"A captain leading an army should have a steed to ride upon," said Yanazume as he handed the reins to Shirō.

"I am unworthy of such a beautiful gift," said Shirō. "And, anyway, I would prefer to walk alongside the other men."

"Well, you have no choice, as I insist," replied Yanazume. "If you prefer to walk, you may lead him. He is a faithful companion. He will serve you well."

And so, on that morning of the second day of the fourth month, the day that commemorated the passion and death of Iesu, seven hundred Christian *samurai* from the region began the long march from Hitoyoshi to Yatsushiro. They would be joined by others along the way. With them they carried white standards bearing a bright red image of the cross. As Shirō had articulated in the conference of *daimyō*, they hoped that such a show of force might lead to some form of negotiation with the army of Tokugawa. At the very least, they would request safe passage for all the women, children, and the elderly. But, if need be, they would engage the army of the *shōgun* in order to save their brethren from starvation.

As they reached the southern edge of Watari close to Shirō's home, they stopped to water the horses, as well as give the men a chance to eat something. Though it was a day of fasting, they had to acknowledge the need to stay strong in body. On the rising slope to the right of the path stood the old Usenji temple, the very one Shirō's grandmother had frequently visited. It was large for a countryside temple, and was constructed in such a way that it appeared to be jutting out from the hillside. With its sloped roof lines and elongated form, the temple's upper level reminded Shirō of a painting he had once seen of the ark of Noah upon the mountain of Ararat.

Outside the temple, an old *bonze* paced back and forth. For a moment, it looked as though he might walk down to the path, perhaps to inquire as to the purpose of such a large force marching upon the open road. But he simply turned away and walked back into the temple.

After a short time, the low metallic sound of the temple bell reverberated through the air. It arrested the attention of everyone, even the horses. The sound diminished and another identical one rang out to fill the empty space.

From the exits of the temple, armed men poured out and formed a line stretching along the hillside. The line advanced forward as more men emerged and formed yet another line. The process repeated until the lines were, by Shirō's estimate, thirteen deep, a force larger than the Christian army. And the enemy had the high ground.

When Lord Onizuka learned of the plan to send soldiers from Hitoyoshi to aid those in the fortress, he dispatched troops under the command of Lord Ikeshita to intercept them. The old temple in Watari would serve as a tactical base from which to launch the ambush. As it turned out, Usenji had harbored the very *sōhei* warriors who had aided the Christians in the winter. The commandeering of the temple would also serve as a form of retribution against the resident *bonzes*, whose ultimate fate would be decided later.

As the Christian army observed the formation of the force now looking down upon them, Tomi placed a hand on Shirō's shoulder and spoke a single word, "*Uragiri.*"

"What does the letter say, Your Grace?" The secretary wanted to read it for himself, mainly because he knew his own Latin to be better than that of the bishop's. But the letter was still in his superior's hands.

"Ah, yes, well," the bishop cleared his throat. "It reads as follows...

Greetings to Your Eminence, the Bishop of Macau.

I deeply regret the expulsion of your priests from my country. Understand that this decision was ultimately made by my uncle, acting supreme military commander, with the support of a majority of the feudal lords throughout the islands. It is my sincere wish that I might have intervened to allow the priests to remain and minister to the vast number of converts they have helped to gain in the name of Iesu Kirisuto. Alas, such action would have resulted in increased conflict and, I fear, more bloodshed. I do humbly request your prayers on behalf of the Christians here, and indeed for all the people of my country...."

The bottom of the page was stamped with the official *inkan*, the royal seal, of the Empress Meishō.

"Is that all, Your Grace?" The secretary had a slightly puzzled look.

"Ah, yes, that is the gist of it." The bishop opened a locked drawer of his desk and placed the letter inside.

"It just seems a bit curious to send a personal courier so great a distance to deliver such a terse message." The secretary was about to ask to see the letter, but the bishop had put it away before he had the chance.

"Yes, well, I suppose we'd better send him back with at least the courtesy of a reply." The bishop opened an unlocked drawer containing stationery. He removed a clean sheet and took hold of a quill from its stand. He began to write.

Her Imperial Majesty, Empress Meishō of Japan,
   I thank you for your correspondence. Please be assured of my prayers for you and all the people of your islands.
   Yours most sincerely, Jorge Maldonado, Bishop of Macau

"Martim, if you could transcribe that into Japanese for me." The bishop handed the letter to his secretary. "And feel free to add anything you think might round it out a bit more."

"Yes, of course, Your Grace, but…"

"That will be all, Martim. I have much that requires my attention today." He looked at the courier, who had been standing silent the entire time. "And see to it this man gets a proper meal, yes?"

"Of course, Your Grace."

A line of archers on the hillside took aim and loosed a volley that fell like a hailstorm into the army from Hitoyoshi. Those standing on the open road began to drop like overripe fruit from the vine. Voices shouted, "Take cover!" Men ran for the line of trees on the river side of the path, many dragging wounded companions along with them. Behind them, the river was wide and flowing freely.

Shirō took in the situation, and saw that it was dire. For a moment it seemed that everything moved in slow motion, and all sound became muffled. He looked up to the sky, hoping to see some sign from Heaven itself. But there were only the clouds. They were stretched and thin. Lowering his eyes back down to the earth, he found himself filled with a sense of despair. It was not for himself, but for those souls sealed up in the fortress. He had set out upon a mission to save them, and now that mission would fail, just as his mission to save the wife of Yoshimura had failed. And this feeling of defeat only made the despair more acute.

In the midst of the chaos, something caught his attention. Down by the river where the horses were tied, the banners of the cross fluttered in the breeze. Shirō thought about what Iesu had endured on this day some sixteen hundred years earlier. It occurred to him that sixteen hundred years really wasn't so long in the grand scheme of things. As he gazed upon the simple shape on the banners, Shirō felt a sense of hope and courage well up in him. He understood that he had nothing to fear because Christ had already won the victory. Shirō knew that, for his own part, he only needed to stand on the same side as the victor. He clutched the cross around his own neck and whispered, "Lord, thy will be done." Then he began to run toward the river.

The head of fire danced its way over the ground and disappeared into the great crevice beneath the wall. Lord Onizuka and the others watched it with clenched anticipation. Then there was nothing. Onizuka leapt down from his horse and began to shout, "Fools! Did you not run the powder all the way..." Before he could complete his question, there was an explosion like a great belch from the earth.

The Englishman, the one called Anjin, had once told Onizuka of how a castle wall in Britain had been brought down by the explosion and subsequent fire ignited by the fat of pigs. Though he had an ample supply of gunpowder at his disposal, Onizuka had been curious to test this method. He'd been skeptical, but could now see just how combustible the stuff really was. The wall, already compromised by the pounding of cannon fire, collapsed in a smoldering heap. A sickly smell of rancid meat filled the air. With large portions of two of the fortress walls now reduced to rubble, the armies of Tokugawa came rushing into the grounds like a relentless tsunami wave.

Reaching the water's edge, Shirō untethered Takeo and sprang into the saddle. The animal was unsettled by all the noise and commotion, but Shirō spoke softly to him and caressed his mane. Riding over to the place along the shore where the banners stood, Shirō took hold of one by the long wooden pole to which it was affixed. With his free hand, he made a sign of the cross. Then, with a firm kick of his heels into the horse's sides, Shirō rode off away from the scene, back in the direction of Hitoyoshi.

Tomi had been busy with his bow. Despite the range and difficulty of firing uphill, he had managed to take down a few of the enemy. Once his quiver was empty, he availed himself of the abundance of arrows strewn upon the ground. He and many of the others had seen Shirō ride off. Some thought perhaps panic had simply gotten the better of him. Tomi knew that wasn't the case, but he nonetheless wondered what his young friend was up to.

The soldiers of Tokugawa had been slowly advancing down the hill. With the Christians greatly outnumbered and hemmed in, they would be easily mowed down or forced into the river. Some of the Christians with bows were proving pesky, and the captains commanding the hillside decided it was time to charge. But just before the order could be given, a loud cry was heard coming from the direction of the temple.

All heads instinctively turned toward the sound. At first its source could not be identified, as all eyes looked to the grounds and entrances of the temple building. But attentions were arrested by a waving motion and a bright white shape against the gray sky. A man mounted upon a snowy horse was on a large rock outcropping at the top of the hill beside the temple. He bore a tall banner emblazoned with a cross of crimson. Waving the banner high above his head, he shouted down, "You who would have us trample upon the image of our Lord, behold! I lift it high where no foot may reach it!"

One of the commanders cried out, "I will make a captain of the man who brings him down!" This caused a wave of excitement among the troops. A line of men wielding Dutch muskets came forward and took aim.

From its position behind the trees, the Christian army observed the enemy advancing down the hill. But the soldiers came to an abrupt halt as their attention was diverted back in the direction of the temple. What Tomi and the others saw next was astonishing. At the top of the hill, upon a large slab of stone above the temple, was their captain seated upon his horse and waving the banner of the cross. He was shouting loudly, though they could not clearly make out his words.

The entire army of the enemy seemed momentarily spellbound.

Then Tomi spotted a line of men wielding muskets take aim at Shirō.

One of the enemy soldiers shouted, "One shot at a time! Otherwise we won't know whom to promote!"

A roar of laughter erupted from the soldiers. Several shots were fired, but the man on the horse did not yield his position. He continued to wave the banner and shout with greater intensity. The fourth musket shot struck the edge of the rock, sending shards of stone in all directions. Takeo reared up but Shirō did not let go of the banner. He fell back and landed hard upon the stone, as the horse scrambled to the security of the hillside.

Shirō stood up, quickly raised the banner, and continued to wave it. In the next instant, he felt a searing pain penetrate deep into his left side. Doubling over, he dropped to his knees.

The soldier knew he'd hit his mark the moment he saw the young man slump over. It was a clean shot and he was rather pleased with himself. As he turned to receive the praise of his comrades, he was startled to see an unfamiliar face bearing down on him. The final thing he felt was Tomi's blade through his belly.

With the enemy troops distracted by Shirō's unbridled display, the Christian soldiers had dashed out from the treeline and raced up the hillside into hand-to-hand fighting range. With skill and singularity of purpose, they quickly turned the tide of the battle.

Tomi fought his way up the hill to the outcropping where Shirō lay motionless. He knelt beside his friend and saw the bright red stain on his left side. Shirō looked at Tomi with an expression that was almost apologetic before his eyelids began to flutter. Tomi clasped his hands around Shirō's shoulders and said aloud, "Oh, no you don't!" With that, he lifted Shirō and carried him to Takeo, who stood patiently at the rock's edge.

As they raced back in the direction of Hitoyoshi, Tomi held the horse's reins with his right hand, while keeping pressure on Shirō's wound with his left. "Stay with me, old friend," pleaded Tomi, as he kept Shirō propped up in front of him. "We'll be there soon."

Shirō saw to his right the river, flowing fast in the opposite direction. His mind reached back to a time when he was twelve years old. He and his father had taken a boat down the river to visit relatives in Sakamoto. On the way, they camped one night on a narrow beach. It wasn't necessary, but Hiromu wanted to spend the time with his son, who was growing up all too quickly.

As the two sat by a small fire, they ate *onigiri* that Shirō's mother and Obāsan had prepared, and a few *ayu* fish they had caught earlier from the boat.

"Papa," said Shirō, "do you believe we will see each other in Heaven?"

Hiromu was taken slightly off guard by the unexpected question. "Well, I certainly hope so. Our job is to make sure we get there."

"*Hai*," answered Shirō.

"And," added Hiromu, "our job is also to help each other get there."

"Do you think Obāsan will be in Heaven?" Shirō had

been troubled when he learned that baptism was necessary for salvation. He wondered about all those he knew and loved who had not been receptive to The Way.

"Well, that is a question I cannot answer. This is why we must constantly pray for others, and do what we can to guide them toward truth."

"What do you suppose Heaven will be like, Papa?"

"I can't say for certain, but I imagine it is more wonderful than anything we can imagine."

"I sometimes fear it may be quite dull. I mean, if we're merely spirits floating around for all eternity..."

Hiromu laughed. "Dullness results from a lack of something. In Heaven there is nothing for which we shall want, so you needn't concern yourself with such a thing."

Shirō recalled that on the few occasions he had complained of boredom, Obāsan chided him saying, "Those who grumble about being bored reveal more about themselves than about their situations!"

Hiromu asked, "Can you recall a moment when you felt a sense of total happiness?"

Shirō thought about that. He did recall one summer when they visited a family friend in the fishing village of Tanoura along the coast. Late in the afternoon, Shirō had hiked alone to the top of a mountain, upon whose slopes grew *mikan* oranges and *nashi* pears. It took him nearly two hours to reach the top, but when he did, the view of the sunset over the bay was breathtaking. There was a moment, so fleeting that even his memory could scarcely capture it, that he was filled with a sense of peace and a perfect joy that, had it lasted any longer, might have brought him to tears.

"*Hai*," said Shirō, answering his father's question.

"I believe moments such as these are perhaps little glimpses of Heaven."

"Perhaps we're having one of those right now, Papa."

Hiromu smiled and tousled his son's hair. "Perhaps we are!" Then he added, "And don't forget, we won't be just floating spirits forever. When Our Lord comes again, we will be reunited with our physical bodies."

Shirō remembered a talk he'd had with Father Olivera about the doctrine of the resurrection of the body. Shirō found the idea incredible, yet it made sense that if man was created as flesh and spirit, he was destined to return to that intended united essence of being. Death, decay, and separation from the body were conditions of a fallen nature. But Iesu united his divine nature to our human nature so that even our bodies might one day be glorified.

"Shinpu says it will be a perfected body," said Shirō.

"That's right," replied Hiromu. "Imagine a body not susceptible to any kind of illness or injury...a body free of any flaw or imperfection."

Shirō pondered that for a moment. "I guess that means, if Obāsan gets to Heaven, she won't need to correct my posture."

Hiromu let out a roar of laughter.

Shirō heard what he thought was the voice of his father. But it was Lord Yanazume. "Ishibara-san tells us you saved many lives today."

Shirō looked around and realized he was back inside Hitoyoshi Castle. There was a sharp pain in his side, and he was weak from loss of blood. Still he managed to speak. "Perhaps, but not the ones we set out to save."

Lord Yanazume replied, "You mustn't blame yourself. Despite our most sincere efforts, not all can be saved. We save the ones we can, and that is what you did today."

Shirō had been laid down upon a straw *tatami* mat. Lord Yanazume's own physician was at hand, but there was little that could be done. The lead ball had bored deep and become lodged in the spleen. Tomi knelt at Shirō's side, and took his friend's hand. "Greater love than this no man hath, that he lay down his life for his friends."

Shirō turned his head, a small flash of surprise in his eyes. "You're quoting the *Seisho*."

"Yes, well, you quoted it so often, I took it on myself to read a bit. I just couldn't admit it to you."

"Continue to read, Tomi-san. There is wisdom and life in the words."

"You know, I should be the one lying there."

"No, Tomi, there is still more for you to do here. One thing I ask is that you watch over my family. I know this is no small request."

"It would be my honor."

Shirō winced as he attempted a smile. "Just perhaps leave the carrying of *suika* to someone else."

Kumiko had been there when they brought Shirō into the room that served as an occasional makeshift infirmary. She fought hard to hold back her tears, as she did not want the sound of her wailing to be the last thing her husband heard in this life.

Though Shirō was not yet aware of her presence, there was also another woman in the room. In the opposite corner, Michiko had been resting on a *futon* when Shirō was carried in by Tomi. Though weak with fatigue, she had been roused by the sight of her wounded son. She managed the strength to call out. But it was not Shirō's name she called. Rather, it was the name of her daughter-in-law. "Kumiko-san, *chotto onegai shimasu.*"*

Kumiko moved silently and knelt down beside her mother-in-law. Michiko whispered something. Kumiko nodded and left the room.

Shirō, now alert to his mother's presence, turned his head to look upon her. She met his gaze with a smile of assurance, but there was a profound sorrow deep within her eyes. With some effort, she turned over and propped herself up with her forearms. She then crawled toward the place where her son lay. Tomi moved to assist her, but realized there was little he could do, as she did not make any attempt to stand. Having made her way to her son's side, Michiko gently stroked his hair and laid her head upon his chest.

After a short while, Kumiko came back into the room. She was accompanied by Lady Yanazume. Each of them held something securely in her arms. They knelt down beside Shirō, and Lady Yanazume said, "Onīsan, meet your baby brother and sister."

Shirō's eyes widened as his pain seemed to leave him momentarily. He whispered, "*Futago.*"

"*Hai,*" replied his mother. Reaching up to touch the child held by Lady Yanazume, Michiko said, "This one I will call Maria." She then motioned to Kumiko to hold out the baby swaddled in her arms. And that one, I believe I will name him…Masaru."

Shirō smiled. "I wish I could stay long enough to play with them. There is much I would like to teach them."

"They will learn all about their big brother. As for play, I think they may wish to play with you right now." Shirō reached out to touch the infants, and each of them grabbed

---

* "Please assist me."

a firm hold of one of the fingers on either of his hands. He felt their gentle squeeze and rubbed their tiny hands with his thumbs.

As everything in the room became dim, Shirō began to feel himself fade. He sensed his mother leaning over him. The warm drops of her tears upon his head brought him back to the moment of his baptism.

EPILOGUE
あとがき

In the privacy of her chamber, the young empress sat at a low table. She read again the letter brought to her by a secret courier. She knew that she had placed the man's life at risk by sending him to deliver her message to the bishop in Macau. She had first composed a draft of the letter in her diary. She knew even her uncle would not make such a bold intrusion upon her privacy. And if he did, so be it.

Her secret study of Latin had enabled her to produce the final letter that would find its way to the bishop. She was most disappointed by the terse nature of his reply. She wondered if perhaps he had simply been prudent not to say more than he had. But she wondered also, given the outcome of events at Yatsushiro, whether he had taken any measures at all. Every living soul in the fortress had been slaughtered and beheaded. Even those already dead from starvation and sickness had their heads taken. The bodies were left to rot where they lay, while the heads were displayed along what portions of the walls that remained. This was to serve as a warning to any would-be converts or insurrectionists.

The empress read in silence the second paragraph from

the draft of her letter to the bishop of Macau. It was the part of the letter the bishop had not read aloud to his assistant. It was the part he had chosen to ignore.

Your Grace, I have learned that the shōgun, *my uncle, has contracted with the Dutch for one of their ships to attack the old fortress on the bay of Yatsushiro. I know what I ask is much, but I beg you to use your position and influence to somehow prevent this from happening. I am no military strategist, but perhaps a blockade using Spanish ships might dissuade the Dutch from going through with a commission to which I believe they are not wholeheartedly committed in the first place. Those inside the old fortress—men, women, and children—have devoted themselves to Iesu, and now they suffer in his name. I beseech and pray that you do whatever is in your power to bring them aid.*

The empress closed her diary and removed a beaded cord from the folds of her *kimono*. She looked upon the image of a man nailed to a wooden cross and spoke, "God of the children of The Way, the one called Iesu, though I do not know you, I desire to know you. I failed to stop the expulsion of your priests from my land. Without the sacraments of your church, I fear the people will wander in spiritual darkness. Those with earthly power have cast you out from these islands, yet I pray you will show mercy. Please do not abandon those who believe and desire to walk in your friendship. I shall pray each night for your return to these islands of my ancestors, even as I pray that their souls may someday look upon your face. I ask for the grace to pray also for those responsible for the murder of the innocents. Though difficult to do so, it is what you have commanded."

With that, the empress made a sign of the cross with her right hand and began to pray.

終

AUTHOR'S NOTE

After graduating from the University of Montana in 1996, I spent the next four years teaching English in Kumamoto Prefecture, on the island of Kyūshū in rural southern Japan. Among the myriad ways in which the people and culture there enthralled me, the devotion of the small but tight-knit Catholic community was something that captivated my interest. In retrospect, I recognize that devotion as one of several factors that rekindled the flame of my own lukewarm faith at that time.

My years in Japan were life changing for many reasons, not the least of which was meeting the woman who would become my wife. It was a blessing that my parents were able to fly over from the States for the wedding and subsequent trip to Nagasaki. I'm probably one of few people who can say he got to spend his honeymoon with his parents in tow. Nagasaki is, sadly, best known as one of the two cities destroyed by atomic bombing. Somewhat ironic is that Nagasaki and Hiroshima were both cities with some of the highest concentrations of Christians in Japan.

Despite the historical images of destruction, Nagasaki today is a vibrant and beautiful—I'd even say, romantic—city adorned with parks and scenic views overlooking the harbor. In addition to visiting the Nagasaki Peace Park and Atomic Bomb Museum, we also discovered the Twenty-Six

Martyrs Museum and Monument. It was here that I came to know the story of St. Paul Miki and his companions, who were crucified on Nishizaka Hill in 1597. For the sake of storytelling, that particular event in Masaru was placed in closer proximity of time to the events leading up to the uprising of Christian peasants.

During my most recent visit to Kyūshū, my wife and I took a ferry ride from her hometown of Yatsushiro to the nearby island of Amakusa. This became a sort of pilgrimage as we visited some of the sites significant to the history of Christianity in the region. Shortly after disembarking from the boat, we came to a place at the water's edge where a bronze statue of a young man with a ponytail stands mounted upon a huge stone. On his lower body, the man wears the swords and *hakama* of a *samurai*. On his upper body, he dons an ornate shirt with a large piccadill collar, in the fashion of early 17th century Europe. In his outstretched hand rests a dove. The man and the creature regard one another in an eternal stare.

The statue is the likeness of Shirō Amakusa, the young Catholic *samurai* who is the inspiration for the main character in Masaru. The family name of Nakagawa was borrowed from my Japanese maternal grandmother. The real-life Shirō did indeed lead an uprising of peasants, many of whom were persecuted Christians, in what came to be known as The Shimabara Rebellion.

The actual rebellion, which lasted from December 1637 to April 1638, took place on the Shimabara Peninsula of Nagasaki, just north of Amakusa. Visitors today can see the ruins of Hara Castle, the fortress where some thirty thousand people, including women and children, sought refuge. In Masaru, the setting of events was shifted slightly eastward, primarily between Yatsushiro and Hitoyoshi on the main island of Kyūshū. This is the area more intimately familiar to me, having lived there for a considerable time. But those wishing to learn more about the actual events will find themselves directed to points northwest of the setting in Masaru.

On our visit to Amakusa, we also visited the Amakusa Christian Museum, a site dedicated to the history of Christianity in Japan, and the Shimabara Rebellion in particular. It was here that we saw on display the Portuguese banner described in Masaru, the one with an image of angels adoring a consecrated host. It was this banner that inspired me to develop a story about the rebellion and its young leader.

Research quickly led me to discover that relatively little is known about the real Shirō Amakusa. An online search is likely to lead one to anime, manga, and video game characters of the same name. We know he was a young *samurai* whose family was Catholic. He probably studied medicine on the island of Amakusa where he was born. In Japan, it's still fairly common to see family names that coincide with geographical place names. It is a matter of historical record that he led the ill-fated rebellion that ultimately ended with the execution of every person within the walls of Hara Castle. Shirō himself was also beheaded, as he never actually left the fortress grounds following its occupation. Over time, several supernatural events have been attributed to Shirō, including miraculous healings, even walking on water. Though none of these have been approved by the Church, it is fair to say that the person of Shirō Amakusa has served as an inspiration to Christians in Japan and elsewhere.

One miracle connected with Japan that does have Church approval is that of Our Lady of Akita. This miracle involves Marian apparitions and a wooden statue of the Blessed

Mother in northern Honshū. Witnesses have reported tears flowing from the eyes of the statue. There is a passing reference to such an occurrence in Masaru, though I would encourage readers to learn more about Our Lady of Akita.

Following the events of the Shimabara Rebellion, Christianity in Japan was strictly banned for nearly two and half centuries. With the arrival of Commodore Perry in 1853 and the subsequent reopening of Japan to the outside world, foreigners were once again permitted into the country. French Catholic missionaries were astonished to discover an entire community of "hidden Christians" in Nagasaki. This underground group had, albeit without the benefit of ordained priests, baptized and handed down the faith to their children over the course of all those generations. When news of this reached the West, Pope Pius IX declared it a miracle.

I was recently asked whether it was true that the empress of Japan at the time of the Shimabara Rebellion was a secret disciple of Christianity. Sadly, there is no evidence to suggest that this was the case. The idea was inspired by the person of Shinzō Abe, recent prime minister of Japan and the first Catholic political head of state. It does seem plausible, however, that given the survival of Christianity in Japan for so long a time, someone was surely offering up prayers that were eventually answered.

—Michael T. Cibenko

GLOSSARY

Amaterasu: Celestial sun goddess from whom the Japanese imperial family claims descent.

anō, eeto: Interjections conveying hesitation, much like "umm" or "hmm" in English.

aoi no gomon: Tokugawa family crest, consisting of three encircled hollyhock leaves.

arigatō: Thank you.

Asa no misoshiru o tsukutte kuremasenka?: "Will you make my morning miso soup?" A traditional proposal of marriage.

ayu: Small salmon-like fish.

baka: Fool.

bakana: Stupid; pointless.

bangohan: Supper. Literally, "evening rice".

bonze: Buddhist monk.

bunraku: Form of theater utilizing puppets with exaggerated facial expressions.

bushido: Samurai code of chivalry.

butsudan: Display containing an image of the Buddha.

chanko nabe: A hearty stew commonly eaten in large quantities by sumo wrestlers as part of a weight-gain diet.

Chanto kīte iru no?: Hey, are you paying attention?

chibikko: Term of endearment for a small child.

chō: Distance of about 350 feet.

chōbu: An area of about 2.5 acres.

Chotto onegai shimasu: Please do me a small favor.

Daijōbu yo!: I'm alright!

daikon: Variety of radish with a long slender white root.

daimyō: Feudal lords and vassals of the shōgun.

Deru kugi wa utareru: "The nail that sticks up gets hammered down." A proverb meant to convey the dangers of non-conformity.

Dete ike!: Get out!

Dōmo arigatō: Thank you very much.

dōzo: Expression of offering, akin to "Please, help yourself."

fukuin: Gospel. Good news.

fumie: Bronze tablet bearing the image of Christ or Mary.

fune: Boat.

futago: Twins.

futon: Quilted mattress laid out on the floor for sleeping.

futsukayoi: Hangover.

gaijin: Foreigner. Literally, "outside person".

geisha: Hostess trained to entertain men with conversation, dance and song.

genkan: Entry way to a home or other building where one customarily removes shoes.

genpuku: Coming-of-age ceremony marking the transition from child to adult status and the assumption of adult responsibilities.

gyūdon: Rice topped with cooked beef and onions.

hai: Yes.

Hai, daijōbu: Yes, I'm alright.

Hai, dōzo: Yes, by all means.

Hai, wakarimasu: Yes, I understand.

Haite mo ii desu ka? Is it alright to enter?

hakama: Loose fitting trousers still worn today by some martial arts practitioners

han: Estate of a daimyō.

hashi: Chopsticks.

hashigo: Ladders.

hayaku: Quickly.

hinoki: Cypress; tall, slow-growing tree valuable for the lumber it produces.

hira oyogi: Breaststroke.

hon'ne: Sincere depth of concern.

ichi-man: 10,000.

iie: No.

Imjin Wars: Japanese invasions of Korea (from 1592–1598).

inkan: Official stamp of identification.

inoshishi: Wild boar.

Itte kimasu: I shall return.

jingasa: A head covering with a domed peak. Literally, "war hat."

jishin: Earthquake.

kabuto: Helmet with a horn-like projection.

kabuto mushi: Rhinoceros beetle, so named because its head resembles the kabuto, a helmet with a horn-like protrusion.

Kampai!: Cheers! Literally, "Empty the cup!"

kanzashi: Long thin stick for holding in place a woman's hair or ornament.

katana: Sword characterized by a curved, single-edged blade with a circular or squared guard and long grip to accommodate two hands.

kawasemi: Kingfisher bird.

kendama: Children's toy consisting of a long handle and a cup to which a ball is attached with string.

ki: Energy or life force of a living being.

ki: Tree. Also a homophone for word meaning energy or life force.

kimono: Long, loose robe with wide sleeves and tied with a sash.

koi nobori: Carp-shaped windsocks traditionally flown for particular celebrations.

koma inu: Statue pairs of lion-like creatures that guard the entrance of some shrines.

kotsuage: Ceremony in which the cremated remains of a deceased are passed with chopsticks from one family member to another and placed into an urn.

kōyō: Changing colors of the autumn leaves.

masaru: Victory.

matcha: Type of green tea made from leaves that have been ground into a fine powder.

mikan: Small seedless orange.

mikazuki: Crescent moon.

mino odori: Literally, "raincoat dance," a form of execution by which one was adorned with a coat of straw, doused in oil, and set alight.

misogi: Shintō ritual cleansing beneath running water.

moku: Wood.

musume-san: Honorable daughter.

naginata: Halberd-like weapon.

nashi: Asian pear.

Natāru: Christmas, from the Portuguese "natal," meaning "birth".

nehan: Nirvana.

ni-man: Twenty thousand.

obāsan: Grandmother.

Obon: Buddhist festival honoring the spirits of deceased ancestors.

Ohayō gozaimasu: Good morning.

Ojama shimasu: Polite expression when entering someone's space (literally, "I commit an intrusion.")

ojīsan: Literally, "grandpa," but used to address any elderly man.

okāsan: Mother.

onigiri: Rice packed into a ball shape, often wrapped with a sheet of dried seaweed.

onīsan: Honorable expression for older brother.

otōsan: Father.

pan: From the Spanish and Portuguese word for "bread." Still used in modern Japanese.

ri: Unit of distance equaling about two and a half miles.

ryokan: Inn with baths.

sai: Dagger with two prongs curving outward from the hilt.

sanka: Obstetrics.

Sei...no!: A command given for all to act in unison, somewhat like, "Heave, ho!" in English.

Seisho: The Bible.

senbei: Rice crackers, often served with tea to guests.

Sengoku: Literally, "warring states period," a time of near-constant civil war and unrest (from AD 1467 to 1615).

seppuku: A form of ritual suicide by disembowelment, also referred to as "hara kiri".

shaku: Unit of linear measurement, a little less than a foot.

shamisen: Stringed instrument, similar to a banjo.

shimarisu: Chipmunk.

shingaku: Theology, literally, "heart learning".

shisei: Posture; manner in which one holds himself.

shishi-nabe: Wild boar stew.

Shizuka ni!: Be quiet!

shō: Measure of volume, equal to about half a gallon.

shōchū: A hard liquor distilled from rice or sweet potatoes.

shōga: Ginger root.

shōji: Sliding interior door.

sōhei: Buddhist monk warriors.

suika: Watermelon.

sukebe: Pervert.

Sumimasen: Sorry; Please forgive me.

tabi: A sock with split toes for easy wearing of sandals.

taishō: Military rank equivalent to general.

taketombo: Children's toy consisting of a thin dowel attached to a propeller for flight.

tanzen: Thick kimono-like garment.

tatami: Compressed straw mats used as floor coverings.

tatemae: Superficial level of consideration.

tono: Lord; master.

torī: Gateway commonly found at the entrance of a shrine.

tsukimi: Literally, "moon viewing," a time for admiring the autumn moon.

tsunami: Tidal wave.

tsuyu: Rainy season of early summer, literally, "plum rain," as it coincides with the season of plum ripening.

ukon: Leafy plant known for its medicinal uses.

uposatha: In Buddhism, days of rest in conjunction with the lunar phases.

uragiri: Betrayal.

ushō: Specialized fisherman who uses trained cormorant bids to catch fish.

uzumimon: Small, often hidden, entrance in a fortress wall.

Wakarimashita: Understood.

wakizashi: Shorter companion sword to the katana.

yabanjin: Barbarian(s).

yagura: Turrets of a castle or fortress.

yakata: Loose-fitting one-piece cotton robe.

zabuton: A padded floor cushion.

CPSIA information can be obtained
at www.ICGtesting.com
Printed in the USA
LVHW030042100223
739114LV00003B/266